A THUN

By the same authors in Pan Books

SEED OF STARS

A THUNDER OF STARS

DAN MORGAN AND JOHN KIPPAX

PAN BOOKS LTD
LONDON AND SYDNEY

First published in Great Britain 1974 by
Pan Books Ltd, Cavaye Place, London SW10 9PG

ISBN 0 330 24098 6

Printed in Great Britain by
Hunt Barnard Printing Ltd, Aylesbury,
Buckinghamshire

Alert for the new, stubborn landing,
Strong-sinewed in armour and might,
In brotherhood, see earthmen banding,
The bringers and guardians of light.

Here, we work close together, or perish
On new lands a lifetime from home;
All other men's skills we must cherish,
All other men's hearts are our own.

There is no clear trail of man's making
Across all the black angry years;
There is only the sound of forsaking,
There are only the traces of tears.

Long past is the pioneers' trailing
To Jupiter, Venus and Mars;
Now we leap from old Sol Three failing,
And we flinch at the thunder of stars.

Ivan Kavanin.

Honoured Poet of Earth.
(2065-2148)

THUNDER OF STARS

Sex can be regarded as having certain therapeutic and recreational values. However, when a relationship between male and female crew members is prejudicial to the maintenance of good order and discipline, it must end forthwith.

(MANUAL FOR SPACE CORPS OFFICERS P. 54 Revised Edition 2160)

TOM BRUCE slept as relaxed as a cat, his lean body stretched naked beside her. A few feet away, on the bedside table, Helen Lindstrom could see the glow of the tiny pilot light on his communicator, could hear the hiss from the tiny loudspeaker, a constant link with patrol HQ. Behind her, on the other side of the bed, her own communicator hissed likewise, giving an occasional splutter when the present sunspot activity made itself felt. This was the measure of their privacy. Neither was ever *off* duty. The Corps demanded their total allegiance, and would go on demanding until there was no more to give.

Realizing that sleep would not come unaided, she eased herself from the bed. She was halfway to the door when the light came on. Bruce, raised on one elbow, was watching her.

"Why not tell me about it?" he said quietly. His green eyes were alert, his lean face attentive.

Then he *had* noticed. She stood quite still in the

middle of the floor as he surveyed her big, cream and gold body. Now she would have to tell him, revealing a more fundamental nakedness.

"Statues?" He grinned briefly, then picked up a thin dark cigar and lit it.

With a slight shrug, she came back to the bed. "The Commissioning Board," she said.

He drew on his cigar. "What are you worrying about? You've got it made. I gave you a good report."

"I expected that you would." She lowered herself to the foot of the bed and sat looking at him.

"This is what you've always wanted, isn't it? Second in Command of *Venturer Twelve*."

"Of course, but . . ."

"But what, woman?" He rose to a sitting position, his lean body suddenly tense, the outline of the scar on his left cheek pale against his tan. "It wouldn't have got as far as a Commissioning Board interview if they weren't sure you could handle the job. Carter and Suvorov don't waste their time."

Helen looked steadily at this lean, hard man with his severely regulation-cut, rust-colored hair and his hard green eyes. She felt a growing tightness in her stomach. He had never said anything about love, neither had she.

His eyes were looking through, beyond her now, out into the vastness of space, and his voice was almost wistful. "You'll be going farther than any human beings since the beginning of time. New worlds, beyond the imaginings of the prophets."

"No, Tom—I shan't be going," she said.

"What do you mean, for God's sake?"

She looked away, unable to face the hardening of his green eyes. "I've decided not to take the post. Four, perhaps five years away from Earth . . . away from you."

"*Me*? What in hell's name has that got to do with it?"

She hesitated. It had to be said now, but she was suddenly afraid.

"This is the chance of a lifetime for you," he said, rising from the bed and walking across to the clothes closet. His wakefulness was now the kind which made further sleep impossible.

"I love you, Tom," she said.

He turned, his hard, scarred face startled, as if he had been struck. "*Love*?"

"Is that *so* incredible?" she said. "We've been together now for more than two years. Surely that must mean something?"

"Of course it means something," he said. "We've had two good years, and that's more than either of us had a right to expect; two years during which our relationship was fortunate enough to coincide with the interests of the Corps."

"The Corps . . . ?"

From anyone else, such a speech might have sounded pompous, a posture—but she knew this man; knew him as a lover, and as an officer. Tom Bruce did not spare himself, or anyone else, in the course of his duty to the Corps. He meant every word. He was getting dressed now, putting on the uniform of Lt. Commander Thomas Winford Bruce, 556396, Commander, Solar System Patrols, but in his mind he never took it off.

"You're prepared to give up everything you've worked for because of an itch in your belly? You realize that if you refuse this you'll never get another chance?"

"I happen to think that you're worth that much of a sacrifice," Helen said. She knew it sounded banal, but it was the truth.

He stared at her for a moment, as if she were a total stranger, then he said: "Blast you! Blast you to hell! You talk like some sloppy, sub-navel-thinking female with a minus I.Q. *Sacrifice*! For God's sake! You've no right to try to saddle me with that!"

Helen tried desperately to cancel out the mistake. "I didn't mean it that way . . ."

"You meant it *just* that way," Bruce said.

He fastened the top button of his pale blue uniform jacket. In some lights, and with some expressions, you could call him hatchet faced; he looked like that now. "If the positions were reversed—if I were the one who was going to the Commissioning Board tomorrow—what do you think *I* would do?" he said.

The answer was so obvious that she ignored the question. At heart, he was a "deep space" man, discontented to be confined to the task of policing the "back yard" of the Solar system—even though that back yard comprised billions of cubic miles of space. In fact, he was the obvious choice for commander of a ship like *Venturer Twelve. He had been the obvious choice for Venturer Eleven.*

"I'm sorry, Tom. I've made a mess of it," she said, looking up at him. "I *am* your woman."

"You *were* my woman," he said. "Now it's time for you to remember that you're Lieutenant Lindstrom." He moved toward the door. "Dockridge will collect the rest of my gear tomorrow."

Fighting back the urge to run after him, she stood quite still as the door closed.

RADIO MESSAGE (OPEN)
COLONIZATION SHIP ATHENA TO EXCELSIOR CORPORATION.
MESSAGE 5 SHIP TIME 1700.

ALL PASSENGERS NOW THROUGH FIRST DRILLS. SETTLING IN FOR HYPERSPACE BREAKTHROUGH PROCEEDING. SHIP SPEED .1 LIGHT. Lacombe, Capt.

THUNDER OF STARS

Twinkle, twinkle little star,
Does your planet have a bar?

(SPACEMAN'S PRAYER : Trad.)

IN THIS early morning session, before the Admiral's arrival, Susan Pringle extracted from the cryptic (frequently almost illegible) scribblings on the pad what she interpreted as his wishes.

At this moment she was talking by vidphone to the civilian foreman in charge of the steelmen who were engaged in the construction of *Venturer Twelve*. The subject of the conversation was Carter's note: "Stupid bastards overloading A.G. lifts—*big stick*!"

"Yes, Mr. Foran—the Admiral quite understands that your men are on a tight schedule," she said, smiling sweetly at the forbidding granite face of the foreman. "But he is insistent that it would be best if more attention were paid to observance of safety regulations."

"Hell! Lieutenant, these men are professionals," Foran protested. "They know the risks involved if they cut a few corners here and there."

Sue Pringle stepped up the wattage on an already considerable charm. "Mr. Foran, *my* Admiral's name is Carter—*not* Nelson, and his vision is twenty-twenty. Make life easier for us both, huh?"

Foran's expression melted gratifyingly. "Well, all right, Lieutenant. I'll see what I can do."

"That's all I ask," purred Pringle. "Thank you, Mr. Foran. Good morning." Cutting the vid, she looked down again at the scribbling pad. The next item read: "Commissioning Board, re Lindstrom. What the hell is Mariano trying to pull?" That, she decided, was one for the Admiral's personal attention.

Next came the name VELMA, in large capitals, underlined three times. Pringle smiled quietly to herself—another personal item. She must remind the Admiral that his wedding anniversary was due in two weeks' time.

"Engine Linings—V12. Call Chalovsky." She extracted this one, placing it on her own memo pad.

"M/F balance of crew. Maranne—too dammed sexy?"

The outer door opened and Rear Admiral Junius Farragut Carter, O.C. Explorations Division, Earth, entered.

"Morning, Sue." Carter was fifty-four, squat as a bug, grizzled, leather faced, with a rare smile that, when it appeared, lopped at least twenty years off his age. He smiled now, as he faced his secretary. His blue uniform was specked with lint and stained here and there with patches of oil. His gray hair, such as remained, stood up in a short, irascible fuzz. On his left breast, taking pride of place in the assorted fruit salad, was the black and gold ribbon of the Space Cross. Junius Carter had been everywhere and seen everything.

"Morning, sir," said Sue Pringle, returning his smile with a genuine warmth.

"Anything from the President's office?" he asked.

"No, sir—not yet."

"Hell!" Carter trundled his way toward the door of the inner office. "Come in, will you? There are a couple of memos we ought to get out right away."

Pringle, dark and willowy, topping her boss by about an inch and a half, followed him inside, notebook in hand.

As the Admiral lowered himself into his seat behind the big desk, the outside vidphone beeped. He grunted, and pressed the receive button. The picture of a handsome woman of about fifty appeared on the screen.

"Junius! There you are!"

Carter's face wrinkled like an abused walnut. "And just where did you expect me to be, Velma? On the tiles with a blonde? Or do you figure I spend all my time in bars?"

"Junius Carter," said his wife, determinedly. "You have not been home in eight days. I'm thinking of suing you for divorce, and naming that damned ship as correspondent!"

"Velma, that's a ridiculous—"

"It is not! Before this one, it was *Venturer Eleven*, and before that it was *Venturer Ten*, and . . ."

"Dammit, Velma!" barked Carter. "Be reasonable!"

But the voice that had made thousands leap to attention had no effect on Velma Carter. "Junius, I have been married to you for thirty-two years and I'm tired of being reasonable. You promised years ago when you got this Earth-based job that I would see more of you. But it just hasn't worked out that way, has it? You're like a little boy with a big constructor set, building those flattened eggs that go into space. As soon as you've done one, you're on to anoth—"

"That is not so!" Carter averted his attention briefly from the screen and saw that Pringle had moved round toward the wall where the power link for the vidphone was connected. She was waiting, poised, for a signal.

"You said that you were going to retire . . ."

"Subject to the exigencies of the service."

"The service," opined Velma Carter, "is just too damned exigent. The truth about you is that you like playing spaceman. If you don't—"

It was at this point that, in response to a twitch of Admiral Carter's eyebrow, Lieutenant Pringle's dainty foot moved swiftly, disconnecting the power plug of the vidphone. The picture vanished, leaving a blank screen. All was peace, save for the distant grind of operations in Shipyard Seven.

Carter gave his pps a guilty glance. "Thanks, Pringle. But we can't go on doing that."

"I'll have a word with the main switchboard," Pringle said. "Perhaps some new directive on the subject of personal calls?"

"My wife is a very determined woman."

"I know, sir."

"She'd take it up with World Admiral Hoffner, or even with the President, if necessary."

"I know, sir."

Carter shrugged. "Maybe we'd better leave things as they are." He looked up at his secretary, his craggy face suddenly serious. "I still love her."

"Yes—I know that too, sir," Pringle said. Her smile was affectionate. She raised her notebook. "There was something about a memo?"

The admiral bared his teeth as he stared up at the big chart that filled half of one wall. The chart showed every post that had to be filled in the commissioning of *Venturer Twelve*. There remained only a few blank spaces; the rest contained the name and number of a corpsman or woman. The two most significant blanks were at the very top of the pyramid of command.

"Yes . . . a memo," Carter said. "Confidential, to Admiral Suvorov. 'Sam: What the hell is this business about Lindstrom for Second in Command? She wasn't even rated in preliminary discussion. Imperative you see me before meeting.' "

"Helen Lindstrom?" Pringle said.

Carter nodded.

"A first-rate officer; what's wrong with her for the job?"

Carter blew out his leathery cheeks.

"I've managed to work with the Commissioning Board fairly well, considering that Sam Suvorov is the only real spaceman on it. Mariano, Yow Thin Thang and Ericson are all admin types; they never flew anything bigger than a mark three desk in their lives. All right, I'm prepared to tolerate that, if they're going to start playing politics . . ."

"Politics?"

"Oh, come on, Sue, don't tell me you haven't recognized this as a typical piece of Mariano finagling," Carter said. "Second in Command of *Venturer Twelve*—any one of a dozen officers would suit. But there's only one man for the job of Captain—the obvious choice."

"Lieutenant Commander Bruce?" Pringle said.

"Of course."

"I still don't see that the possibility of Helen Lindstrom's getting the Second in Command job constitutes any barrier to Bruce's being Captain," said Pringle.

"I just hope you're right, Pringle," said the Admiral. "But I have my doubts. I can't see Mariano backing down that way." He glanced up at the wall clock. "Anyway, we shall find out in about an hour's time."

He rose and walked to the window, where a strong sun glared through the slats of the blind. From there he could see the great silver bulk of *Venturer Twelve* dominating the lively complex of a thousand skills which made up the shipyard.

A gentle smile played about Sue Pringle's lips as she watched him.

THUNDER OF STARS

Let me talk to ships; and out to planets
Where human seed, precariously sown,
Takes watchful root on alien ground.

(TELECOMS : I. Kavanin)

THE ELEVATOR doors opened silently and Bruce stepped out into the great, vaulted chamber that was Main Control, the nerve center of System Patrol. Dominating the room from its position in the center was the macro-simulator, a transparent globe enclosing a three-dimensional reproduction of the Earth/Luna system, with Earth as its center, and Luna near the outer limits. Scattered in seemingly random pattern throughout the interior of the globe were upward of a hundred pinpoints of light, varying in color and intensity, some steady, others blinking in bewildering oscillation. Each pinpoint of light was a ship going about its business within a radius of three hundred thousand miles from the center of Earth.

Ranged around this central focus were tiers of desks and control consoles, each with its batteries of screens constantly monitoring a sector of space. Behind each of the first row of consoles sat headphoned crewmen or women, watching the screens, and talking quietly into throat mikes as they fed a constant stream of data into the central computor that controlled the moving image within the macro-simulator. In the tiers behind, further consoles, linked with scanning stations on planets and in orbit throughout the solar system, monitored space outside the englobement of the simulator, as far as the orbiting trans-Plutonian perimeter stations.

Bruce stood for a moment, looking upward, his mind digesting the information presented by the simulator, then turned as a lean, graying terrier of a man wearing PO's uniform approached and saluted.

"Anything to report, Dockridge?"

"Com systems very erratic sir; sunspots."

"But you're managing to keep an accurate general picture?"

"Good enough, sir, but there's an awful lot of mush."

"Can't be helped."

"Let's just hope we don't get any Class A emergency," Dockridge said. "That could be very slaggy."

"Hm . . . Anything else?"

"Sir?"

"Disciplinary?"

PO Dockridge alerted. "No, sir?"

"On the apron," Bruce said, his eyes boring, "Leading Crewman Gleason is walking about smoking a cigarette—saw him as I parked the flycar."

Dockridge shook visibly. "Omigawd!"

"I don't want to see him again," said Bruce. "Just tell him he loses a week's pay and month's promotion, and if he's caught once more I'll have his balls for gyros. See to it, Dockridge, and report to me in my office afterward." He walked quickly away.

The matter of the sinning crewman settled by a terse vidcall to the PO in charge, Dockridge was in the patrol chief's office within two minutes. Bruce was chewing a black cigar as he leafed through the pile of pink and yellow stat copies that had accumulated during his off-duty period.

"Anything here of importance?"

"Just routine, sir."

"Right." Bruce balled the lot in his palms and threw them into a disposal chute. He began reading command orders, then said, without looking up, "When are you going off?"

"In an hour, sir."

"Good. Send a couple of men along to clear the apartment, will you?"

Dockridge frowned. An ordinary run-of-the-mill PO would have merely executed the order and thought no more about it. But Dockridge had worked with Bruce for a long time.

"Leaving, sir?"

Bruce gave him a stony look. "Bright this morning, Doc?"

"And Lieutenant Lindstrom . . . ?"

"Will make her own arrangements."

The corners of Dockridge's mouth turned down. "Not your girl any more?"

"Spare me your advice to the lovelorn. Just get on with it." Bruce produced a yellow corps form and handed it over. "Take this along to billets and see what they can do for me."

"Yes, sir." Dockridge took the quarters application form.

"Oh, and Doc . . ." Bruce said as the PO saluted and turned to leave.

"Sir?"

"It's not quite what you think."

Dockridge allowed himself the merest shadow of a grin. "Things seldom are, sir." He left.

Alone in his office, Bruce turned his attention to the contents of his IN tray. He scanned at a great rate, discarding ninety percent, considering nine and three quarters, and hesitating over the remainder for only a few seconds before noting decisions. Administrative work of this kind was completely undemanding for him, except in terms of boredom. It was only when he was actually out on patrol in his command ship that he really felt he was doing something.

Helen Lindstrom had begun as a casual attachment. They suited each other's physical requirements exactly, that was one thing. For another, she was a fine officer, well balanced and as attentive to detail as he was. She was, in the highest term of praise possible for a corpsman, "All Corps."

"Love," he muttered, "be damned to love." What he had done was for the best—for both of them. And, within a few days, if she passed the scrutiny of the *Venturer Twelve* Commissioning Board, she would be gone, anyway. The next time he saw her after that, *she* would probably be his senior, looking down at him as an old deadbeat who got stuck on the promotion ladder. Unless Carter *did* succeed in working the miracle.

He turned his attention determinedly back to the paper work; then, needing a stylus, he slid open the right hand drawer of his desk.

A pair of fine-quality, dark blue leather gloves, Corps female officers' issue, lay there. Moving with quick irritation, he picked them up, balled them together, and aimed them at the disposal chute.

For the first time in memory, he missed.

He sat for ten full seconds, gazing down at the gloves on the floor. Then, rising from his chair, he walked across the room and picked them up, feeling the soft warmth of the leather.

Back at his desk, he replaced the gloves in the drawer and closed it gently.

Form 3713/2/IRR.
EXCELSIOR COLONIZATION CORPORATION.
IRREGULARITY REPORT.

FROM: Radio Room.
TO: Corpn. President.

MESSAGE 6 FROM COLONIZATION SHIP ATHENA (OUTGOING) FIFTEEN MINUTES LATE. UNABLE TO RAISE, POSSIBILITY OF SUNSPOT ACTIVITY.

THUNDER OF STARS

We are the girls of the old Space Corps
They say we're as good as men.
We'll fight and swear, and drink,
  and whore.
And we'll die—
There's no difference—then . . .

(SONG OF THE
CREWWOMEN—Trad.)

SENIOR LIEUTENANT Helen Lindstrom sat on the edge of a hard chair in the anonymous, cream-painted anteroom of the Commissioning Board. She shifted her shoulder slightly, aware of the chafing of an over-tight strap on her brassiere.

"The Board will see you now, Lieutenant Lindstrom."

She looked up into the smiling eyes of Admiral Carter's pert-faced secretary.

"Thank you, Lieutenant Pringle," she said distantly as she walked toward the door of the inner room. *Damn that bra strap*!

"Please be seated, Lieutenant Lindstrom," said Admiral Carter, who was sitting in the chairman's position, flanked on either side by two members of the board.

"Thank you, sir." She obeyed, then took advantage of a slight pause and shuffling of papers to scan the faces of the board members. Her candidature for the post of 2 i/c *Venturer Twelve* would already have been discussed at length by the board, acting on the data provided by Med/Psyche, Personnel Records and a dozen other departments, but despite Bruce's assurance that "she had it made," Lindstrom knew that commissioning boards were important. About Carter himself she had no misgivings; his bark was notoriously loud and frequently profane, but she knew that he had a true devotion to the ideals of the Corps.

Seated on Carter's right was Admiral Sam Suvorov, a cheerful West African whose graying hair showed strongly against his ebony skin. Suvorov had a mind of his own, but as far as the essentials were concerned, it was safe to place him in a similar category to Carter. She had no such certainty about the dark, sharp-featured Latin on Carter's left. Rear Admiral at thirty-six, Sylvano Mariano had a reputation in the corps as a pusher of the most efficient and ruthless type, an Admin officer and a politician. Next to him sat Yow Thin Thang, a Commander from the South East Asian Area, an unknown quantity; and on the other side of Suvorov sat Commander Ericson, blond and slab headed, with eyes that bored through her like a pair of blue lasers.

"Now, Lieutenant Lindstrom," said Admiral Carter. "All the members of the board are familiar with the details of your career since you joined the corps. These are matters of fact, contained in your record file."

"Which is beyond reproach," cut in Mariano, smiling.

Helen Lindstrom stiffened involuntarily. It was from Mariano, if anybody, that she had expected opposition. That he should go out of his way to be charming at the outset put her even more on guard.

"Good," Carter said, frowning slightly. "Admiral Suvorov?"

Suvorov leaned forward slightly. "Lieutenant Lindstrom, apart from a three-month tour of duty on Perimeter Station 15, you have been based on Earth, have you not?"

"Yes, sir," Helen said. "I have made application on several occasions to be drafted to *Venturer* service."

"That is a matter of record, Lieutenant," Carter said sharply. "Have the goodness not to waste our time by amplifying your answers unnecessarily."

Helen Lindstrom decided hurriedly that this was one of those days that had earned Carter the nickname "Crusty" among the other ranks of the corps. She would have to be more careful.

"But the fact remains that you have never, for any period longer than those three months, been away from Earth?" said Suvorov.

"That is correct, sir."

"You are aware that the tour of duty of *Venturer Twelve*, on this, her maiden voyage, will be at least two years?" Suvorov said.

"Yes, sir," Helen said.

"Lieutenant Lindstrom, are you familiar with the nature of the aberration known as geo-nostalgic psychosis?" asked Admiral Suvorov.

"I have heard of such cases, sir, naturally." Helen was unable to suppress a frown of puzzlement. "But surely there's nothing in my Med/Psyche record to suggest . . . ?"

"Of course there isn't, Lieutenant." This from the chivalrously smiling Mariano. "Your stability rating is excellent. With all due respect, I fail to see the object of Admiral Suvorov's question."

Suvorov's expression hardened. "If the Admiral had experienced the incidence of this psychosis among a crew, he would be more qualified to judge the pertinence of the question. Within the present limits of Med/Psyche investigation, there is no certain way of predicting the vulnerability of a given subject."

"Then why . . . ?" said Mariano.

"Indications are that personnel with long-standing emotional attachments here on Earth are more prone to succumb to geo-nostalgic psychosis, however impeccable their stability ratings," said Suvorov.

Helen maintained her upright position in the chair and kept her facial expression carefully neutral. The interview showed all the signs of developing into a sparring match between the space-going and the admin members of the board, with herself caught in the middle. The bra was pinching now with a vengeance.

It was Admiral Carter who brought the real object of the present line of discussion out into the open, and he did it with his usual well-known lack of finesse, his face dark with either anger or embarrassment, or possibly a combination of both.

"Lieutenant Lindstrom, this board is aware that you have been sleeping with Lieutenant Commander Thomas Winford Bruce for the past two years."

This board is aware. . . . The damned old toad! Helen Lindstrom felt a flush of color suffusing her features. *What the hell had it got to do with him, who she slept with?* This was the woman's reaction, but the officer part of her mind managed to view the situation more soberly and to note with some alarm that Carter, upon whom she had looked as an ally when she entered the room, was in fact an enemy. For some obscure reason of his own, it appeared that he was opposed to her appointment.

"Lieutenant?" Carter barked interrogatively.

"I was given to understand that the board did not require my comment on matters of fact, sir," she said, with dignity. "My relationship with Commander Bruce is now ended."

Carter harrumphed and blew out his cheeks.

"A surprisingly convenient *fait accompli,*" said Yow

Thin Thang blandly. "Perhaps the Lieutenant would like to give us further details?"

Helen was aware of an anger building up in the pit of her stomach.

"I hardly think that would be necessary, or desirable," Mariano said, smoothly. "If the episode is finished, there is no more to be said. Now, Lieutenant, perhaps you would like to tell us how you feel about your ability to cope with this appointment? Does the size of *Venturer Twelve* daunt you? The magnitude of your responsibility?"

Helen raised her chin just a fraction. She sensed that she was on firmer ground now. "I have the Corps with me," she answered. "If I know my job, they know theirs."

Mariano nodded, apparently satisfied.

Ericson asked: "Have you ever experienced any difficulty in the application of discipline?"

She shook her head. "No, sir."

"Then you consider yourself a tough person?" persued Ericson, the blue-laser eyes boring into her. "Tough. Not physically. I can see that, without asking. But how do you react in, say, situations of strain—constant strain?"

She gazed back at him steadily. "I saw some of my documents once—quite by accident. Since then, I've always felt that I had to live up to the reputation they gave me."

Mariano chuckled briefly. "I think that answers your question, Ericson."

From that moment Helen felt able to relax slightly. The questions that followed were merely routine, taxing neither her resources nor her temper. Carter was clearly still under tension, his face wrinkled with bottled-up anger, but the anger was not directed against her and remained contained. He asked her no further direct questions, and when he next spoke it was to make the formal announcement that concluded the interview.

"This board appoints you to the acting rank of Lieutenant Commander, with the position of Second in Command of *Venturer Twelve.* Within twelve months of this appointment your rank will either be confirmed or you will be demoted. You are to put up your new badges of rank for first parade Saturday morning; your promotion will be announced in Corps orders next Friday evening. That will be all, Lieutenant Commander Lindstrom. You may go."

"Thank you, sir," she said, rising to her feet.

Composed and beautiful, she responded to the relaxation of formality as the members of the board came from behind the table and shook hands with her, offering their congratulations. Four of the members of the board. Carter stood, head sunk between heavy shoulders as he stared out of the window across the shipyard toward the gleaming bulk of *Venturer Twelve.* She looked at his broad back for a moment, hesitated, saluted and left.

When she gained the roofpark of shipyard building, she paused for a moment, looking out toward the shining city. With no smoke, and no natural haze on this bright day, the distant hills were clearly visible, purple and enduring, twenty miles away. She took off her cap and the wind tugged at her hair. Behind her, with half a dozen other flycars, stood her own craft, wearing the decorous dark green of all service vehicles. As she looked at it, she thought that, in a week's time, she would no longer have to requisition for one of the pool vehicles; her new rank would entitle her to her own personal transport. She had felt tense, even angry, at the interview. Now that emotion had left her and she was placid. The promotion meant more responsibility, that was true. She could take it. It meant that she could have a crewwoman GD as a servant, her accommodation allowance increased twenty-five percent, her "in space" pay doubled, with an added command pay, while her basic rate increased thirty percent.

It came to her that she had no one with whom to share the success. There were two aunts in Stockholm, a second cousin in Lima, and a brother who was a mining engineer on Mars, a beaver of a man who was content to stay there and let his pay accumulate back home. She could send him a message telling him of her new rank, and then he could send her one in congratulation, and that would be that.

She thought about Tom Bruce. But the time of sharing things with him was past—if it had ever really existed.

She was brought down by the knowledge that, if she were to die at that moment, the most disturbed people in the world would be the men who had just promoted her.

She roused from the mournful deliberations, turned and walked to the flycar. The park attendant was typical of his kind. He had the uniform and pay of a leading crewman, and he limped.

He saluted cheerfully. "I've checked her out, Commander."

She returned the salute. "Thank you." She was about to step into the craft when she stopped. "What did you call me?"

He smiled, almost affectionately. He might have been just old enough to be her father. "I'll paint two and a half bars on the door, ma'am, if you'd like to wait five minutes."

"It's a pool car—but how did you know?" She felt pleasure that he cared, in a mild, general way, that she had been promoted.

"Got a job where you hear things," he grinned. "Soft

job man, now. Time for gabbing." He nodded east, where the silver egg of *Venturer Twelve* rose over the shipyard like a pale sun. "I'm still in the Corps—penguin branch." He was dark and thin faced, with a grin that spread round his sharp nose and touched his black eyes with welcome geniality. "That ship, she'll be yours. And I think about other ships. I was in *Venturer Eight* and *Ten*. I got a young cousin in *Eleven*. Can't leave it alone. Space is like a whore you keep going back to even when you know she's poxed." He moved his left leg with an awkward tug and grimaced. "Sometimes I just stand here and look."

"Your leg?"

"Got shot out of an airlock. Smacked against a wall. Never mind, I make out. They look after us. What price glory, eh?"

"You were in *Ten*. When?"

"When Tom Bruce was Senior Lieutenant."

You can't get away from Bruce, she thought.

"We were in orbit when he and Panos and Dockridge went down to Minos IV. Never knew the truth of that. Shut up like clams, everybody did. And what those things were that they brought up from surface I don't know." His face, which had momentarily looked thoughtful, cleared. "Would you tell Commander Bruce that Ed Dimitrov would like to be remembered to him?"

She smiled at the grounded veteran. "I'll tell him, surely." She climbed into the car, swung it up in the regulation straight lift, and headed southwest, toward the distant gulf lands.

"Gentlemen, the appointment of a commander for *Venturer Twelve*," said Carter. "I'm open to propositions for a short list of possible candidates."

There was a moment of silence, then Mariano said:

"Very well, I'll be the first to stick my neck out, if that's the way you want it. I propose Commander Charles Longcloud, at present 2 i/c Space College, an officer with an impeccable record and the highest qualifications."

"You can spare us the commercial," gritted Carter. He glanced round the table. "Seconded?"

"Yes, I'll second Longcloud's nomination," Ericson said, with a suspicious promptness.

Yow Thin Thang said: "He has done some excellent practical work in the field of system meteor disposal."

"A bloody cosmic trash collector," grunted Carter, but he got the message; three down and one to go. He turned his eyes on Suvorov. *He*, at least, was a *real* spaceman, who knew the kind of man who was needed for such an appointment.

"I agree that Longcloud is to a large extent an unproved man," Suvorov said, gazing into the middle distance. "But there's no reason to suppose that he would reflect anything other than credit on our choice."

"What the hell—?" began Carter.

"On the other hand," continued Suvorov firmly, "at this stage there can surely be no harm done by looking farther afield for our candidate? There must be a number of experienced officers of the rank of Lieutenant Commander and above who would be capable of handling this appointment."

Carter subsided, coming to the conclusion that he had underestimated both Suvorov's loyalty and his subtlety.

"Perhaps Admiral Suvorov had some particular officer in mind?" said Mariano blandly.

Suvorov breathed deeply and stroked his chin. "No . . . I was merely making a general observation."

Carter sat, head hunched turtlelike between his braided shoulders, his mouth half open as he stared at

Suvorov. Sam Suvorov, of all people to let him down like this!

"We can't appoint a general observation to command *Venturer Twelve,*" Carter bellowed. "We need a *man*! And I suggest that the man we need is Commander Tom Bruce."

"Cozy . . . but impractical," Mariano said, shaking his head.

"What the hell do you mean, impractical?" demanded Carter, doubly incensed. It had been agreed that the proposition should come from Suvorov. Why had he backed down? And now, to have Mariano sniping as well. . . .

Mariano said: "System Patrol is a very important arm of the Corps. Surely it would be imprudent to deprive such a department of both its Second in Command *and* Commander?"

Carter glowered at Mariano. He felt as if he was chewing dirt. "So that was the reason for the Prince Charming act," he said. "I wondered why you were taking it so easy on Lindstrom."

"Lieutenant Lindstrom, as we have all agreed, is an excellent choice for Second in Command," said Mariano.

"Only if Bruce is Commander," Carter said. "These two have proved themselves as a first-class team."

"But the team has already been broken up, Junius," Mariano said smugly. "When such a relationship is ended—even between two highly disciplined officers of the corps—there must be some backlog of resentment on one side or the other."

"There's something in what he says, Junius," said Suvorov.

"There are considerable misgivings in certain quarters about the fitness of Bruce for such a command," Mariano said.

"*Certain quarters*!" Carter's rage exploded in a great shout. "What in blue hades is that supposed to mean?"

Mariano was not ruffled. "I'm sure I don't have to remind you, Admiral Carter, of a TOP SECRET file, labeled MINOS IV?"

"That was ten years ago," Carter said. "Bruce was a very young officer, faced with a difficult decision."

"But he took irrevocable action," Mariano said. "*Without* consulting his commanding officer. Surely that weakens any case for him?"

"There are some who would disagree with you there," put in Admiral Suvorov.

"I suggest that the choice of Commander Bruce could very easily bring about adverse reactions," Mariano said. "To have such an appointment revoked, on a presidential level for instance, would be a considerable embarrassment to the members of this board."

Presidential level . . . Carter smashed his fist down on the table. "That does it, Mariano!" he shouted. "I've sat here listening to your sly politicking and your innuendoes long enough. And now you've the bloody nerve to threaten me with presidential intervention! Me! The legally appointed chairman of this commissioning board!"

"Now just a minute, Junius," Suvorov said, gently. "Let's not lose our tempers."

"*Tempers—hell*!" roared Carter. "Nobody pulls that kind of crap on me and gets away with it." He bounced to his feet, swelling visibly.

"Junius—what are you going to do?" asked Suvorov.

"Do? I'm going to see the World President, of course."

Mariano got up hurriedly, his bland features showing concern for the first time. "You can't do that."

Carter's brows came together and he crouched forward. "I can't? Who says?"

"There are correct ways of . . ."

"Damn right there are!" shouted Carter. "Any general rank can go and see the President when he wants—and I'm on my way! Meeting adjourned!"

The door crashed behind him.

THUNDER OF STARS

If any man or woman, regardless of rank, underestimates or overestimates his or her ability, then comes disaster. If I were asked to state the basis of the Corps' greatness I would say it lies in technical skill, in trust of one's fellow men and women, and in humility. Nowhere in the Corps can we afford arrogance, for arrogance is selfish pride, arrogance comes from the delusion that you know best and be damned to the others. We cannot afford the arrogant; their price is paid in blood.

(World Admiral Joseph Hoffner, S.C.
Jakarta Conference May 2160)

HENDRIK PERSOONS, the big, quarter Indonesian, was on the bridge of the *Athena*. His movements were steady: when he turned, it was not hurriedly; when he spoke, it was quietly, slowly, and every outward sign he gave was of a man in control of himself and of the situation for which he was responsible. The piratical takeover of the ship had been a complete success; but it had only been a beginning.

The shutting off of the drive had been easy: a symbolic, impressive act. But it had been very little more than that as far as the progress of *Athena* was concerned. She hurtled through the starry wastes of space like a steel coffin. The ship was not accelerating, true, but the panel in front of him showed that she was still traveling at the velocity of point seven two of the speed of light, out of the solar system. If the giant twin Grenbachs of her drive were not reactivated, she would go on traveling at that speed forever, or at least until she met some cosmic obstacle and disintegrated.

But he was not going to wait for that to happen. The first step was to reactivate the drive, then to begin the maneuver that would bring the *Athena* round in a huge arc, consuming billions of miles of space, until eventually she was heading back toward the solar system. Under normal circumstances, the ship's astrogation officer would prepare a tape which would then be fed into the computer, and under the control of this tape the monstrous engines would bring the ship round in a perfectly calculated course. But the training of a former Second Class General Duty Crewman in the Space Corps did not include instruction on the preparation of astrogation tapes. If Hendrik Persoons was to turn the colonization ship and head her back to Earth, he would have to do so under manual control.

Joe Kolukwe, the thin, quiet African, came into control and walked across to Persoons. Joe knew where he was and what he was doing, but his mind was filled with the awful memory of a surprised crewman pitching dead at his feet. Joe had never shot anyone before, had never, indeed, seen anyone shot, and he felt as though the mark of Cain blazed on his forehead. Joe had agreed that there was nothing to do *but* rise up against Lacombe and his crew and try to get back to Earth; he had taken the gun to use as a threat, imagining that killing could be avoided. More fool he.

As he spoke to Persoons he knew again that he did not like the man. "All of 'em are locked up under guard down there in the cargo holds," he said.

"Good." Persoons grinned and his face became more

Eastern than his ancestry warranted. "Hope they'll like that nice steady vibration when we get the engines going again."

"I've never seen a man change so much, and so quickly," Kolukwe said, thoughtfully.

"Change?"

"Yes, Lacombe," Joe said. "One minute he was the iron captain, tongue-lashing us like a madman, and the next he was practically on his knees pleading."

"Why? What happened?" asked Persoons.

"Somebody told him we were heading back to Earth. After that all he could do was beg me to let him talk to you; something about giving the senior officers parole so that they could help in the handling of the ship."

"He can jumble that idea, for a start," Persoons said fiercely. "As far as I'm concerned, Lacombe and his officers are part of a corporation robbery plot to deprive us of our rights, and *we'll* bring them back to Earth."

Kolukwe's doubt showed in his eyes. Persoons took him by the shoulder. "Weren't we—*aren't we*—right? Didn't your kid die through that damned medico wanting to put her into cryogenic suspension until we reached Hegenis III instead of delaying hyperspace breakthrough and treating her properly?" Persoons believed his own propaganda and he sounded like it. "Didn't we discover that they were sending us out without the full establishment? And didn't that bloody Captain Lacombe refuse to turn back, or even get in touch with the corporation about it?"

Kolukwe, his mind still filled with the memory of the killing, nodded slowly.

"And didn't the rest of 'em on board accept me as leader and trust me to get 'em back to Earth?" A faintly hysterical overtone crept into his voice. "Trust me, Joe, trust me!"

"Sure, Hendrik," Kolukwe said. "If you say so. After all, you've got space training. You know what you're doing."

Persoons turned back to the console and switched the manual controls of the drive to the warm-up position. There was an increase in the clattering of relays, the sound of the Grenbach engines recommenced, coursing through the very structure of the ship like the low growling of two enormous, captive beasts.

"Are we turning?" asked Lesage, who had followed Kolukwe onto the bridge.

"No, not yet," Persoons said. "First we warm up the engines. Then we switch in the gyros and correct spin—*then* we begin to turn."

"Spin?" Lesage queried.

"Of course, spin," Persoons said. "How else do you think a constant gravity situation is maintained on this type ship?"

"All right, all right, so I'm a mudbound Earthie," Lesage said, raising his hands.

Persoons grinned, his confidence reinforced by Lesage's deference. He walked across to the master intercom and pressed the button that would make his voice heard on every loudspeaker throughout the ship.

"Attention please! Attention please! This is Hendrik Persoons speaking. In three minutes, the gyros will begin to cut down the ship's spin, and gravity will gradually drop to zero." The confident sound of his own voice gave him more assurance. "This means that conditions of free-fall will then exist temporarily aboard the ship. To minimize the effects of this condition, all of you who are not engaged in work directly connected with the running of the ship should get onto our acceleration couches and fasten safety belts."

As Persoons switched off and turned away from the

intercom, he saw the thick-set figure of Connor by the doorway.

"It's all right now, priest," he said, sneering. "The fighting is over."

Connor ignored the jibe. His face was quite calm as he came closer and said: "You're really determined to take her in, on your own?"

"Of course, can you think of any alternative?" Persoons said.

"Yes, I can," said the priest. "I've just been talking to Captain Lacombe. He begs you, for the sake of everybody on board, to accept the help of his astrogator and chief officer at least."

"To hell with him and his officers!" snarled Persoons. "I don't *need* their help."

"You can't possibly take this ship right in and land her on Earth single handed."

"I don't intend to. Once we're back in the system I shall contact System Patrol. Commander Bruce will send a couple of scout ships out to guide us in. No sweat, priest."

"Provided all goes according to plan," Connor said. "This is no flycar you're handling. What makes you think you'll be able to keep those engines in balance without any help?"

Persoons' broad face twisted in a malicious grin. "I'll tell you what you do, priest," he said. "You go back to your friend Lacombe, then the two of you get down on your knees and pray to that God of yours that nothing *does* go wrong. Meantime, don't come around here bothering me with your whining—I've got work to do!"

Connor heard the speech out, his face dark with foreboding. "The Lord have mercy on all of us," he said, quietly.

The room was lofty, silent and austerely luxurious. In the center of half an acre of carpet, Henry Fong was seated at a desk several sizes larger than Carter's own. Given an engine, it would have made a good satellite vehicle. Henry Fong was confidential secretary to World President Oharo. Dressed in sober black and white—in a position as high as his, such exterior show as uniform was unnecessary—he was middle aged, slim, lightly brown and quite imperturbable. He put together his slender, beautifully manicured hands and beamed at Carter, who had just steamed in.

"Hello, Junius. I've been watching your progress for some time," said Henry Fong. "I figured you were about ready to blow."

"You've been spying on me?"

Henry tut-tutted. "Spying? What an old-fashioned word!" He produced a box of cigars and offered them. "Sit down, Junius—and *simmer* down."

Carter accepted the cigar, then subsided into a chair which took hold of him as though it needed a symbiotic relationship.

"Mariano?" Fong said.

"Head on," grunted Carter. "The man's impossible! I'm sorry Henry, but I've tried to be reasonable . . ."

Fong's smile was beatific. "Now *that* is something I would like to see *personally*. And the subject of the difference of opinion, Lieutenant Commander Bruce?"

Carter sagged. "How *do* you do it?"

"I have certain psionic talents, shall we say? Plus a multiplicity of technical resources, naturally."

"In other words, you've got spies," Carter said, scowling. "Then you know the bluff that Mariano is trying to pull. It *is* a bluff, isn't it?"

Henry Fong gave the tiniest of shrugs and studied the ash at the tip of his cigar. "That's hardly something I am at liberty to discuss."

"All right, don't discuss it," Carter said. "Just give me an inkling of the President's feelings in the matter."

Fong remained absorbed in his silent study of the cigar, his light brown face as clear of commitment as an egg.

"Look, Henry, I've got a right to know where I stand," Carter growled. "Mariano is brandishing the idea of presidential intervention. Even if I don't believe him, there are others on the board who will, and this is sure to influence any vote."

Henry Fong became brisker. "Let us do some supposing. Suppose that I helped the President with the compilation of a list of candidates for command of *Venturer Twelve*, and suppose, for the purposes of discussion, that the name of Lieutenant Commander Bruce were included on that list."

"Just a minute!" Carter intervened. "I've seen no such list!"

"My dear Junius, don't excite yourself. We are merely *supposing*. To continue—suppose the name of Lieutenant Commander Bruce were included on that list. There would have to be reservations about his eligibility; for instance there was a certain occasion on Minos IV when his actions caused him to be a center of controversy at the highest level."

"Nobody's going to bring up that Minos IV business again," Carter said. "They wouldn't dare!"

"Not in detail, of course," Fong said. "Our friend Mariano well knows the danger he would be placing himself in if he did so. On the other hand, as a skeleton in the closet, a bogey with which to influence members of the Commissioning Board more susceptible than yourself, this could be useful."

"Then he *is* bluffing?"

Henry Fong resumed the study of his cigar. "You are the Chairman of the Commissioning Board of *Ven-*

turer Twelve, Junius. That's for you to decide. But is it really worthwhile sticking your neck out for Bruce when there's a perfectly good man like Longcloud waiting on the sidelines?"

Carter's squat face darkened. "Longcloud? Is that your recommendation?"

"*Recommendation*?" Henry Fong's eyebrows raised. "My dear Junius, I make no recommendations; we are merely *supposing*, remember?"

Carter's face had a purplish tinge as he extricated himself from the affectionate chair. "It won't *do*, Henry!" he bellowed. "Bruce has pulled up System Patrol to the highest standard of efficiency it has ever known; he's hard, meticulous, a first-class planner and organizer. Beside him, Longcloud is an untested, academic nonentity."

"It's a point of view," said Fong mildly.

"One that I insist on putting to the President," Carter said.

"Consider it put."

"No, Henry—this is something that has to be done personally," Carter insisted. "I'm standing on my right as a general officer to see the President."

"I wish you *wouldn't*," Fong murmured.

An expression of puzzlement mingled with Carter's anger. "Why? What's going on?"

"The President is not available," said the secretary firmly.

"Not to anyone?"

Henry Fong's black eyes were like pieces of polished coal. "Bull's-eye, Junius."

"Then he's not *here*?"

"No."

"There was no announcement."

"There doesn't have to be. He's gone on a little trip."

"Guard of Honor?"

"One—World Admiral Hoffner."

"Where?"

"Moon," Henry said, with studied negligence. "One or two new little things there that he wanted to see for himself."

Carter's eyes narrowed. "You wouldn't fool me, would you, Henry?"

"No, Junius," said Fong. "What I have just told you will be on the newscasts within the next day or so. But, until it is, I must warn you to treat the knowledge as confidential."

"Of course," Carter said. "The last thing I heard was that he wasn't carrying out any engagements for—"

"And now," said Fong, "you hear this." He shook his head, seemingly genuinely regretful.

Carter's anger had died a natural death. He stood looking at the bland features of the secretary, realizing that he had been told just as much as was considered good for him, and no more.

"One thing I would say before you go, Junius," said Fong. "The President appointed you Chairman of the *Venturer Twelve* Commissioning Board because he has the utmost faith in your judgment."

"You mean Mariano *was* bluffing?" Carter said.

A flicker of pain passed over Fong's smooth features at the Admiral's lack of subtlety. "I have said more than enough. You must draw your own conclusions and handle your own Commissioning Board."

Carter's face cracked into a grin for the first time during the interview. "You're darned right, I'll handle them—those chair-borne spacemen!"

"Fine, Junius; you do that," said Henry Fong. "Remember me to Velma, won't you? We must get together some time. Good-by."

When Carter was gone, Henry Fong stubbed out his cigar carefully in the crystal ashtray on his desk, then flipped a switch on his vidphone. "Vargas, get me the officer commanding Space College, will you?"

He switched off and turned his attention back to the documents he had been studying before Carter's arrival. Would that political life were as simple as it appeared to somebody like Junius Carter. Dear old Junius, the unregenerate romantic who kidded the world that he was tough and practical.

The vidphone beeped. "Admiral Vanbrugh on the line," said his PA.

"Thank you, Vargas. Put him on. Hallo, Harry!"—this to the prim face of the commanding officer of Space College.

"Good afternoon, Henry," Vanbrugh said. "What can I do for you?"

"I was wondering," said Henry Fong, squaring the papers on his desk with slim, brown fingers, "if you could spare that excellent 2 i/c of yours for a time. We've been having quite a bit of trouble with meteor incidence in the Perimeter Stations area, and the President wants a detailed report. Longcloud seems the obvious man for the job."

"Well, I—"

Henry beamed. "Fine! I was sure you'd be cooperative. If you'll tell him to report to me first thing tomorrow, we can discuss his briefing."

"But, Henry, Longcloud is—" began Vanbrugh.

"An excellent man," said Fong. "Don't worry, the job shouldn't take more than four or five weeks."

"But I understood Longcloud was supposed to be coming up for interview about the *Venturer Twelve* command," said Vanbrugh.

"Oh, *that*," said Fong blandly. "No, I don't think that will be necessary now. I was just talking to Junius Carter, and the whole thing is pretty well sewn up."

"I can't say I'm sorry about that," said Vanbrugh. "I

wasn't relishing the idea of breaking in a replacement for Longcloud."

"Precisely," said Fong. "Well, do give my love to Edna. We must get together some time. Good-by, Harry." He flipped the vidphone off.

THUNDER OF STARS

It is not the duty of Space Corps men or women to die for others; it is their duty to stay alive and save others. This is not just a quibble of words; within it lies the truth that every situation must be judged in Corps terms, and therefore of mankind generally; it implies that Corps personnel can evaluate without panic, can make decisions on their own levels, and know when their decisions must involve more people and higher ranks.

(World Admiral Joseph Hoffner, S.C.
Jakarta Conference May 2160)

BRUCE STOOD on the concrete in front of the System Patrol building, looking out over the Patrol Spaceport. Lieutenants Garcia and Takaki were on their way up the side of number two scout, raised on an anti-grav lift driven by a G.D. crewman. The lift sailed stiffly like a metal magic carpet, up the sixty shining gray-blue meters of the scout, until it reached the long, slant-eyed nose, where a narrow lock hung open.

The lift swayed momentarily to one side, then clamped onto the port. Takaki and Garcia stepped across and slipped, feet first, into the control cabin. The lift detached itself and floated down until it leveled at about half a meter, then gathering speed it skimmed away toward the maintenance workshops. The lock near the nose of scout number two closed.

Bruce glanced at his wristwatch, counting off the seconds to himself. By the time he had reached twenty-five, the scout was already beginning to lift. He nodded his satisfaction. Quietly, with only the faintest of humming from her A/G generator, the dart shape rose, as though drawn by an invisible cord, up into the hazy blue of full morning.

Pulling on his dark glasses, Bruce watched the ship until she was a tiny dot which suddenly spurted a pinpoint of flame and was gone, as her regular drive took over from the A/G. Apart from his own bigger command vessel, only number four scout now remained on the landing area, and she was cluttered with a gantry and swarming artificers. He turned and walked across the baking concrete into the headquarters building.

Helen Lindstrom was waiting for him in his office. He returned her salute and walked across to his desk. "Sit down, Lieutenant—or is it Lieutenant Commander?" he said, opening a box and selecting one of his long black cigars.

"It will be."

"With effect from . . . ?"

"Next Saturday morning. In orders Friday night."

"Uh huh." He nodded. "Congratulations."

"Thanks."

He squinted through the smoke of his newly lit cigar. "Why so sour? Was it rough?"

"You could say that," she said quietly. "Your friend, Admiral Carter, your dear old buddy . . ."

Bruce frowned. "Junius?"

"I'd rather not talk about it if you don't mind," Helen said. "I thought you might want to discuss the subject of my successor as Second-in-Command—System Patrols, I mean." The qualification slipped out before she had time to think about it and realize its implication. She colored.

But Bruce either did not notice or chose to ignore the remark. "Takaki's good. Tough, too."

Takaki, a little Japanese with the wiry body of a twelve-year-old boy and the face of an intelligent monkey. No, not in Tom Bruce's line at all. Helen Lindstrom shifted in her chair as she tried to stifle a stream of bitchy thoughts.

"Yes, Takaki should do very well," she said, fighting to maintain an expression of intelligent interest.

"Very efficient," Bruce said. "I just timed her takeoff in number two. Twenty-five seconds from closing of hatch to lift."

"Efficient as hell," said Helen Lindstrom. She gritted her teeth as she detected the harsh tone of her own voice.

She wondered if, during those few days that remained, she would be able to control the impulse to approach him on a personal level. It was not going to be easy.

"Yes, I think she'll be pretty good on the admin side," Bruce said. He stood with his back to her, looking out over the landing area.

"You've moved out, then," she said. "The apartment, I mean." *Steady, keep it impersonal.*

"Dockridge tell you?"

"Yes."

"I hope he didn't offer any opinion?" he said, turning to face her.

"No, of course not," she said, avoiding his eyes. Will you get Corps quarters?"

"Here."

"What?"

"Couple of rooms in the basement," he explained.

"Meant for a caretaker but never used. Dockridge had it picked out."

Her mask of indifference slipped a little. "You'd told him that you were leaving the apartment—before you told me?"

"You don't have to tell Dockridge things like that," he said.

The explanation satisfied her. "No . . . not Dockridge," she said. "I shall be moving myself, on Friday —to the officers' mess at Shipyard Seven."

"Meet the new chums, eh?"

She thought about that for a moment. A whole new collection of officers and crew, male and female, awaiting her arrival, awaiting such administrative skills as she possessed to begin the process of welding them into something like an integrated ship's company. With no commander yet appointed, the responsibility would fall squarely on her shoulders for the time being. She drew herself upright. "You'll be wanting me to stay on until Friday?" she said.

"Unless you had other plans," he said. "I thought you might spend a bit of time with Takaki—show her the ropes."

"Of course." She rose to her feet and stood facing him, looking full into his green eyes. She still wanted him; she knew that if he had crossed the few meters that separated them and held out his arms she would have fallen into them without a shadow of hesitation.

Then she remembered. "I met Ed Dimitrov. He said he sent his regards."

Bruce didn't have to think. "*Venturer Ten*. Accident with a lock. Prosthetic bungle over his leg."

"Yes."

"A good man. What's he doing?"

"Limping about on a roofpark."

"He could be doing worse. Thanks for telling me."

The intercom on the desk burped urgently. Bruce stepped across and flipped a switch.

"Yes?"

"Weiss here, sir, UFO. We're getting a purple alert from Perimeter Station Fifteen!"

"I'll be right there." Bruce threw his cigar into the disposal chute and headed for the door. Helen Lindstrom was close behind him.

PO Weiss was waiting for them in Main Control, his round, pock-marked face like a lunar landscape with eyes. "This way, sir," he said, ferrying them through the tiers of desks and control consoles toward the operator who was handling incoming calls from Perimeter Station Fifteen.

"I haven't channeled through the main monitor yet, in case it's a false alarm," Weiss explained.

"Let's hope to God it is," Bruce said, his face grim. "What details do you have so far?"

"Station Fifteen thought it was a large meteor at first," Weiss said. "There was no ship scheduled in that sector. Then they spotted the drive. They put out routine identification calls, but there was no reply."

They reached the console, where a pale-faced, dark girl sat listening to the sound that came through her headphones. Her name was Linda Barutz, and she was Dockridge's girl. A tape was running on the console, recording the message as it came in. The girl looked up. "Reception is very bad, sir. I'm only getting about fifty percent."

"The first purple alert in two years and we have to hit it in the middle of a solar storm," Bruce said disgustedly. "Switch in your console speaker, Barutz."

"I'm trying to filter out the interference, sir." explained Leading Crewwoman Barutz. "But I'm afraid that means an increase in distortion." The three people standing round her console listened silently as the dehumanized voice of the Perimeter Fifteen operator began to come through.

" . . . completely ignored our request for identification. In accordance with . . ." The voice faded out completely and was replaced by a sputtering, crackling surge of cosmic mush. Then, after about half a minute, it crept into audibility again. " . . . to within point oh oh one of actual speed . . . identification, but seems to indicate . . . again to contact by tight beam . . . fifteen . . . instructions from . . ."

"Hell!" Bruce exclaimed. "We could stand here all day listening to this firework display and not make any sense of it." He reached across and switched off the speaker. "Weiss! Get her tape of the messages so far and take it down to Lieutenant Suzuki. I want a detailed semantic analysis within half an hour. In the meantime, Barutz can keep listening and recording."

"Condition, sir?" asked Weiss.

"Normal," barked Bruce. "I'm not going to panic the whole damned system on the strength of what we've got so far. I'll think again when I've seen Suzuki's analysis. Right, man—move!" He turned to Helen Lindstrom. "Get onto maintenance and tell them I want the command scout ready—checked."

"Yes, sir," she said briskly, then in a more intimate tone, "you really think this is it?"

He shrugged. "Who knows? It could be."

THUNDER OF STARS

Feed well, little man, and fortify
  yourself,
Against fear.
Drug well (as directed by Med/Psyche).
Use well (but with consideration) the
  woman who wants
To give and take, and with the warm
  ache in your crotch
Go forth to duty station.
Cast a calm eye on dial and meter,
  circuit and control.
Do not believe that you are alone.

(DUTY. I. Kavanin)

ONCE OUT of lane restrictions over Lake Cities, Carter set his course eastward and switched the flycar to automatic. He set up the small worktable and dug an armful of folders out of his briefcase.

Carter's love of the line of exploration ships was even greater than that affection for his work found in the mind and heart of a dedicated engineer. Carter was a spaceman. Grounded these ten years, save for jaunts as far as moon, he never regarded himself as anything *less* than a spaceman, and it was here that his true value as a commissioning officer lay. The comfort and safety of the men who took such ships across the galaxy was a personal thing to him.

He muttered and pondered over his notes. Panos for Warrant Officer on *Venturer Twelve*—surely that would be a good choice. Those anti-grav lifts . . . there would have to be some really crushing discipline if the civilian construction workers didn't toe the line. Radar Lieutenant Yvonne Maranne . . . Why not let Med/Psyche sort that one out? But watch them, because there was a certain school of thought down at Med/Psyche Centre which was pressing for a complete damping of the sexual urge in long-journey space crews. As an old spaceman, Carter believed that male and female sides of a crew should meet and, without infringing duty in the least, get their adjustments in the normal manner. Such sexual freedom had become traditional in the Corps. He had been pleased to note that World Admiral Joe Hoffner had come right out and said so in a recent public speech.

Joe Hoffner, on Moon with the President. Funny, that—and Fong covering up, for what? The President had gone to Moon, to look at installations; what installations? The only new installations on Moon in the last five years had been some alterations in the sewage recycling system, and that had been last November.

With a small, irritating thought buzzing in his mind like a mosquito, Carter put his papers to one side and glanced down at the neatly quilted agricultural plain that was rolling beneath the flycar. After a moment's inaction, he thumbed the button on his vid and got in touch with Pringle.

"Good afternoon, sir," Pringle said. "I'm getting a terrible picture of you I'm sorry to say."

"Don't bother to say," Carter replied. "I always look like this. Anything urgent?"

"Nothing, sir. Test beds aren't quite finished with the engines yet; a little more checking to do. I said to carry on—they're not holding us up. Right?" She smiled.

"Right," Carter said, with a twinge over his lost youth, regretting that *now* there should come along a girl with so much brain and beauty. "Now listen, Pringle. I want you to locate Karl Hurwitz."

"The surgeon-general?"

"That's right."

"Running a temperature, Admiral?"

"Cut the sauce," growled Carter. "Where did you last hear of him?"

"There was a shot on the news a few nights ago showing him in a trout stream near a village called Invercuckie, Aberdeenshire, Scotland. Do you want I should haul him out of his waders?"

"Just locate him," Carter said. "I'll do any hauling."

"Now?"

"If not sooner." Carter cut the contact.

Fifteen minutes later Pringle was on his screen again, wearing a puzzled look. She shook her head. "I don't get it."

"He's not there." It was more of a statement than a question.

"Left two days ago, they said. Oh, and I had to pretend to be his daughter before they'd say anything. There was a Mrs. MacTavish who was very positive with her negatives." Pringle looked wondering. "You knew?"

"I guessed," Carter said. "Thanks, Pringle. I'll be about twenty minutes." He broke contact. It gave him no satisfaction at all to confirm that he had been right. Henry Fong *was* covering up something, something concerning an old man whose guiding hand was of the utmost importance to Earth and her colonies. Some said he was the main unifying influence which held together a mankind now scattered among the nearer stars; Oharo—tenth president of United Earth.

James Connor, the United Christian priest, formed a natural focal point as he moved among the *Athena* colonists with a cheerful word, a blessing, a comforting hand. He gave of himself unstintingly, and now that they were irrevocably committed by the action of an extremist minority, he offered no opposition to that minority or reproach for what they had done. Soon—once contact was made with the perimeter stations—help would come, and the *Athena* would be guided by the ships of System Patrols.

Meanwhile, they gathered round him, asking questions to which, if they gave the matter a moment's thought, they must realize he had no more certain answers than themselves, and finding comfort in his platitudes.

"My Hendrik did what he thought best, Priest Connor," said Nini Persoons, her small Eastern face solemn.

"Of course, my child," said Connor.

"You will speak for him when the time comes?"

"I will speak if they will listen to me," Connor said. "A priest has little power in the world of affairs." He felt a surge of pity for this tiny girl who had tied her destiny to that of Hendrik Persoons, who would always be involved in violence and unrest, wherever he went. The man was a near psychotic, Connor had guessed that from the start, but now he was certain.

When the gyros had been restarted and the gravity was sufficient to permit controlled movement, Connor had gone to the bridge to find out what progress was being made. There he found Persoons, just roused from a coma of exhaustion, dosing himself with Duty One capsules.

"Persoons, how many of those things have you taken in the last twelve hours?" he asked.

The Eurasian rounded on him, his broad cheekboned face grim, eyes blood-flecked slits. "I don't know—five, maybe six. What's the difference?"

Connor was startled by the admission. Two, and at the most, three Duty Ones was the maximum dosage within twenty-four hours. Like all such stimulants, Duty One created no energy; it merely made available that which already existed in the body of the subject. And once used, that energy had to be paid for, replenished by nourishment and sleep if the subject was not to suffer permanent damage to his system. Persoons, with his Space Corps experience, must have known this perfectly well.

"We're on course for the solar system, aren't we? Why not rest now?" Connor suggested.

Persoons' lips drew back from his strong, yellowed teeth. "You'd like that, wouldn't you, priest? For me to get out of the way and let you take over."

"I was merely . . ." Connor began to protest.

"Sondergaard!" called Persoons. "Get this sniveling Bible puncher off my bridge and take him back to the women and children, where he belongs."

"Yes, Hendrik." The tall Swede took hold of the priest's arm and began to lead him toward the door.

"And Sondergaard!" bellowed Persoons.

The two stopped and turned. The Eurasian was standing now, arms akimbo, his face filled with a new, fanatical light as the drug capsules poured their stimulation into his system.

"If he gives you any trouble, shoot him!" Persoons ordered. "I will have discipline and a complete obedience!"

Outside in the corridor, Connor turned to Sondergaard. "How long has he been like this?"

"It's been getting worse, ever since the takeover," said the big Swede.

"He's quite mad—you understand that?"

Sondergaard shifted uneasily. "Maybe . . . but we're

completely dependent on him. He's the only person who can handle the ship."

"There are still Lacombe and his officers," Connor pointed out.

"For God's sake!" Sondergaard put his fingers to his mouth. "If he hears you making suggestions like that, he'll shoot us both!"

Secretary Fong raised one slender brown hand. "All right, Commander Bruce. Spare me the technicalities. Just tell me this: assuming that we are dealing with a hostile, alien ship, how long have we to prepare ourselves?"

Bruce's hard face remained steady in the desk vidphone screen. "If the UFO maintains present course and speed, it will reach Earth's orbit within, say, twenty-four hours."

Henry Fong glanced at the wall clock. Twenty-four hours to the most important meeting in the history of mankind, and President Oharo was on Moon, already under sedation. *Well, Henry, you always wanted responsibility.*

"I suppose you're quite certain that this couldn't be some kind of false alarm?" he said. "What I mean is, who have you got out there on Perimeter Station Fifteen?"

"The station is manned by three carefully selected units of Space Corps personnel, in the final phase of their officer training."

"Of course, Commander, of course," Fong said. "And how soon can we expect positive identification of this ship?"

"Within an hour, at the latest."

"And if that identification is hostile?"

"Then I shall notify a Red Alert."

"After first informing me, as the President's representative."

"That is the procedure, sir." Bruce's face was impassive.

"A Red Alert entails the grounding of all ships, disruption of trade and transport. It could be expensive for you, Commander, should it prove a false alarm."

"Even more expensive for all of us, if it isn't," Bruce said calmly.

By God, Carter's right, thought Fong. This is a cool one; prepared to make his own decisions, and to stick to them.

"Quite so, Commander," he said. "Keep me informed. Is there anything else?"

"One thing, sir. If this is a Kilroy ship, I want presidential permission to go out there and meet it."

"But surely there are already patrol ships in that sector?"

"System Patrol has six ships, sir," Bruce said. "Four of those are in space at the moment, and only one is any nearer to the sector concerned than Earth itself—and then only a matter of a few thousand miles."

"Even so, Commander, it seems to me that your job is at headquarters."

"Command ship carries the heaviest armament of all, and she's ready," Bruce said. "In this situation, she is the obvious choice."

"We'll talk again when you've received positive identification from Station Fifteen," Fong said firmly.

"Yes, sir."

"Oh, and Commander—"

"Sir?"

"I appreciate your motives for wanting to be first out there. But even if this is a Kilroy ship, we can't be absolutely certain that their intentions are hostile until contact has been established."

"I doubt if they're on a pleasure trip, sir," Bruce said. His face faded from the screen.

In other words, *screw you, sir*, thought Henry Fong. He smiled quietly to himself. Bruce was not afraid to voice his opinion, he had confidence in his own judgment. It was a comfort to have such men around at a time like this.

He leaned across and switched on the internal vid. "Vargas! Get me Admiral Hoffner on moon, will you? Top secret and scramble!"

THUNDER OF STARS

Things ain't bad here,
Don't get me wrong.
But you could have died on Earth
And saved the fare.

(COLONISTS' LAMENT : O Kritz. 2135)

ELKAN NIEBOHR, President of the Excelsior Colonization Corporation, had the reputation of being an honest man. Although well aware that such labels could be of dubious value, after certain investigations of his own Henry Fong had come to the conclusion that, in this instance at least, the majority opinion was relatively correct; that is, provided one did not dig back too far into the man's past. There had been times, back in his earlier, struggling days, when Niebohr had been known to cut a few corners here and there, to bend the law a little to his own advantage. Fong found these past failings not the least disturbing. What Elkan Niebohr had done in the past he would not do again; now a man of tremendous wealth and power, he had no need of such methods. Therefore, in the only meaningful sense as far as Fong was concerned, Elkan Niebohr was an honest man. Q.E.D.

"Hallo there, Henry! Nice to see you!" Like everything else about him, Elkan Niebohr's smile was big. He was massive, with a large, hooked nose, and almost bald.

"Elkan!" Henry Fong's smile was, for him, comparatively uninhibited. He admired professionalism in any field. "How are Jane and the kids?"

"Kids!" boomed Niebohr. "Don't spoil my digestion this early in the day, Henry, please."

"What can I do for you, Henry?"

"There's been something of a panic on at Patrols," Fong said. "One of the Perimeter Stations spotted a UFO headed into the system and raised a purple alert."

Niebohr's big form stiffened. "Aliens?"

"That was the big question, of course," Fong said.

"*Was*?"

"Yes. It turns out that the ship is a Goddess-class freighter. We haven't been able to make radio contact with her yet, but data so far indicates that she's one of your colonization ships, the *Athena*, and she's in trouble."

"*Athena*—she's supposed to be on her way to Hegenis Three," Niebohr said. "Gregory Lacombe in command; he's one of our best men."

"Yes, we have all details of crew and passengers," Fong said. "On the face of it, they're just a mixed bag of colonists bound for a virgin planet. As we haven't yet been able to make direct contact, I was wondering if there was anything helpful you might be able to tell me at this stage?"

Niebohr's dark eyes were guarded. "You mentioned trouble; what kind of trouble?"

"Well, obviously things aren't quite as they should be, otherwise she would have answered the identification calls from Perimeter Station Fifteen," Fong said. "Also, there's something about her drive being out of phase. I'm not a technical man myself, but I understand that can be serious."

"You're darned right it can be serious," Niebohr said. "But I don't understand how it could happen with a man like Lacombe in charge. What action has been taken so far?"

"The System Patrol Commander is on his way now."

"To do what?"

"I take it that the first priority will be to make some kind of contact," Fong said.

Elkan Niebohr's monolithic face was as inscrutable as Henry Fong's bland, oriental features. They eyed each other, through the medium of their vidphone screens, like two powerful, well-matched beasts, each waiting for some move from the other.

"But you have a theory, don't you, Henry?" Niebohr said, at length.

It was Fong's turn to shrug. "There are several possibilities, of course. But there is one in particular that seems to fit the facts, as we know them so far . . . especially since you have confirmed my data on Captain Lacombe. Even if he did encounter some kind of engine trouble, he would hardly be likely to turn back from his scheduled course, and he would most certainly not ignore a request for identification from a Perimeter Station. This being so, I can only assume that Captain Lacombe is no longer in command of the *Athena*."

Niebohr nodded. "Have the CSC been notified of the situation?"

"So far, there is no reason to suggest that this is any of their affair," Fong said smoothly. "But, of course, when the return of *Athena* becomes a matter of public knowledge, then the committee will no doubt feel it necessary to make some inquiries. I'm sure that you have nothing to conceal, Elkan, but there are certain radical elements on the committee who would like nothing better than an opportunity to discredit an organization as big and respected as the Excelsior Corporation. I hope I don't need to be more explicit?"

"No, Henry, indeed you don't." Elkan Niebohr allowed himself the relaxation of a smile. "Thank you for calling. I'll start the ball rolling right away and let you know immediately if anything unusual turns up."

"And I, in turn, will keep you in the picture with regard to the patrol operation," said Fong. "Good-bye Elkan." He switched off the vidphone, reflecting that it was a real pleasure to deal with a man like Elkan Niebohr, whose motives he understood.

"Hear what he's saying!" Lesage squealed. "The ship's going to blow up!"

Persoons' anger returned. "That isn't what I said at all, you stupid cloddie! Now listen! The engine compartment is sealed off from the rest of the ship, as any idiot knows, so even if it blows to hell and gone, the passenger and crew sections should remain intact. But there *could* be a certain amount of radiation hazard. That's why I suggest you move our people."

"Will do, Hendrik," Kolukwe said. "But if the engines blow out, how do we get back to Earth?"

"We put out a call to the Patrol, and they send out a couple of scouts with magnetic grapples to guide us in," Persoons said. "It's been done dozens of times with crippled ships."

"Then why not cut out both engines right now and make a call, without taking any further risks?" Kolukwe asked.

"Because I'm in charge here!" Persoons gritted. "I've brought the *Athena* this far, and I'm going to take her the rest of the way, if it's humanly possible."

Kolukwe faced the broad, implacable features of the Eurasian. It was clear to him, at least, that anybody who disputed Persoons' right to control the ship would have to be prepared to fight to the death; and for Kolukwe there had already been too much blood.

"Sure you are, Hendrik. We'll do as you say." He

turned to the silent Lesage. "Come on!" They walked out of the compartment.

Alone on the bridge, Persoons moved back to the control console. *Stupid cloddies!* They knew nothing, and it was impossible to share his burden with them, to explain to them that there was at least a fifty-fifty chance that before the engines blew, the vibration of their opposing force could breach the hull of the ship—or to explain that despite the fact that the engine compartment was sealed off from the rest of the ship, there was always the chance that the force of the explosion might be channeled inward rather than out into space.

There must be a way . . . there had to be. To have come so far, to have sacrificed so much, and then to fail was unthinkable. His hands began to creep over the controls, making tiny, hopeful adjustments.

PO Dockridge swung into System Patrols Main Control, looking like a terrier rooting for rabbits in undergrowth. He wore a blue zipsuit and his cap was on the back of his head. He was complaining as he came through the door.

"This had better be urgent. A man of my age has to watch his beauty sleep. There was I, dreaming of my wild colonial gel, when. . ." He fetched up against Weiss, who was staring at the transparent globe of the macro-simulator. "Is the boss up?"

"Uh-uh," Weiss said, pointing to a blinking red dot that was nearing the orbit of Moon and would soon be passing out of range of the simulator. "Number Two is with him."

"What's the bug?" Dockridge asked.

"Goddess-type freighter coming in on sector RQ365, reported by Station Fifteen," Weiss said. "No communications contact with her so far, and it looks as though her drive is out of phase."

"Nasty!" Dockridge said. "And Bruce is going out to meet her?"

"That's the general idea."

"Anyone else?"

"Ships Two and Three are on stand-by—but he's going to see what he can do alone, first." Weiss grunted as the red dot reached the edge of the simulator and winked out. "We'll have to follow him through planetary relay now." He turned to where Linda Barutz was hunched over a control panel. "You getting anything from Moon?"

Barutz jabbed a finger at the blurred screen to the right of the panel. "If you call *that* anything," she said disgustedly.

Dockridge frowned. "Damned solar storms! Wouldn't you know we'd get an emergency?" He slid a hand over her shoulder, momentarily possessive.

A loudspeaker on Weiss's console broke into life, relaying the voice of Leading Crewwoman Sharon, who was monitoring messages from Perimeter Station Fifteen.

"Station Fifteen reports estimated speed of freighter as .302 Light, and increasing; .302 Light and increasing."

Dockridge exhaled explosively. "Did I say emergency? You had a course analysis on that thing yet, Weiss?"

"Perimeter and planetary stations are working on it now."

"Blind O'bloody Reilly, they'd better be," Dockridge said. "At those speeds, it may be later than we all think!"

THUNDER OF STARS

We'll find a planet all of our own,
With no one there to annoy us.
No long-range receiver or radiophone,
No alien bugs to destroy us.
We'll live us a life of love and ease,
Devoted to high-level beauty,
Till some silly crug with his mind
  full of cheese
Turns up and starts talking of duty.

(SPACE CORPS DITTY)

SEATED BESIDE Tom Bruce in the control cabin of the command scout, Helen Lindstrom gasped as the estimated speed came through her headphones. She turned to her companion. "Did you hear that?"

"I heard," he said flatly, studying the dials and scopes in front of him. He moved his hand farther back on the throttle control, and Lindstrom felt the surging pressure of high G as the command scout leaped forward, barreling faster and faster into the spangled blackness.

"I've been thinking," Lindstrom said. "We can't be absolutely sure, until we've made radio contact, that this thing really is an Earth-based ship. What I mean is, if the Kilroys were to send one in, they'd do their best to make it look like one of ours, wouldn't they?"

Bruce flashed her a brief, wolfish grin. "Welcome to the club," he said. He pressed a red clip, and a flap fell, revealing the firing buttons of the six missiles that were the command scout's heaviest armament.

"I think we're getting near enough for me to try direct radio contact," she said.

"Go ahead," Bruce said. "We could use some light conversation."

"The trouble with you, Joe, is . . ." Persoons stopped talking as he sensed an abrupt leap in the amount of vibration coursing through the hull of the ship. Swinging his chair round he saw that the dials that registered the thrust generated by the Grenbachs had suddenly gone crazy. His hands flew to the controls and then stayed rigid and impotent with ignorance. The screaming vibration continued to climb in pitch.

A screen on the communications panel lit up, revealing the wide-eyed face of Bose, one of the colonists who were now in Cargo Hold One.

"Persoons! Kolukwe! What's happening? Down here it feels as if the ship is going to fall apart any second."

"Keep those damned cloddies out of my hair!" Persoons snarled over his shoulder.

"What do I tell them?" Kolukwe asked. Two more screens were now live on the communications panel, one showing a male face, the other female, and both were begging for explanations.

There was no reply from Persoons. Head bent over the control console, he was oblivious to everything but the subject of his concentration. Kolukwe used the communications panel camera/mike, composing his features carefully. At all costs he must preserve an outward impression of calm. The faces on the screens were near panic, and he could hear the sound of angry voices as others, out of range of the cameras, shouted to their spokesmen.

"Friends, there's no need to be alarmed," Joe Kolukwe said. "We're on course for Earth, and everything's under control."

"Persoons, where is Persoons?" demanded the dark face of Bose. "We want to hear what he has to say about that."

"Persoons is busy," Kolukwe said. "You'll just have to take my word, for the time being."

"What about the vibration? It's like living inside a circular saw," protested a pale, haggard-faced woman, speaking from Hold Number Three. "The children are frightened, and nothing we say seems to calm them."

"The vibration will pass," Kolukwe said. "Persoons is working on it."

He went on, pacifying them, trying to instill in them a confidence that he did not feel himself: promising them a safe end to their journey and a quick release from the screaming tension generated by the vibration of the drives. Eventually he was successful; the screens flickered off one by one, and he was once more alone on the bridge with Persoons.

He turned and saw to his astonishment that the Eurasian had swung his chair round, turning his back on the flashing red lights and madly climbing needles of the control panel, and sat watching him.

"We'll make a politician of you yet, Joe," Persoons said with a slant-eyed grin. "You handled them just fine."

"What are you doing, Persoons?" demanded Kolukwe. "The controls. . . !"

"Useless—there's nothing more I can do," Persoons said. "The master circuit has blown."

"*Nothing* you can do?"

Persoons shrugged. "Without a skilled maintenance crew, not a chance. The engines are building up into a runaway reaction; they'll just go on until they burn out."

"And then what?" Kolukwe asked.

"It could be worse," Persoons said. "At least we're on course for Earth."

"But we can't make a landing without engines," Kolukwe said. He thought about the crew, imprisoned down there in the holds.

"Bright, real bright," said Persoons as he approached the communications panel.

"So what are you going to do?" Kolukwe asked.

Persoons said confidently: "I'm going to call System Patrols and dump the baby in their lap. It's time these fancy-uniformed bastards got to earning their keep."

"I don't see . . ."

"Right, cloddie—*you* don't see," Persoons said contemptuously. "So I'll explain. Like we might not be able to land with our engines out, but we're headed in the right direction, and a couple of Patrol ships latched onto us with magnetic grapples could easily maneuver us into orbit. From there it would be a simple matter to ferry our people down to Earth."

Joe Kolukwe felt a surge of relief. They were going to get back after all. But following close on the relief was the nagging certainty that, even when they got back to Earth, their troubles were a long way from being over.

Beyond the orbit of Jupiter, and heading outward fast, Bruce sat in the control seat of the command scout and listened to the gutturally accented voice that was coming through the small loudspeaker over his head. Beside him, Lindstrom too listened, her face pale and strained beneath her helmet as she began to understand the enormity of the situation, as she thought of the women and children on board the hurtling *Athena*.

"Record everything," Bruce said. "And try for a picture as soon as possible."

"Yes, sir." She busied herself with the communications controls. Reception was bad, blurred intermittently by splashes of static caused by solar activity.

Bruce used his microphone, cutting in on the voice from the loudspeaker. "Now, Persoons, I want you to tell me, as clearly as you can, just what has happened aboard the *Athena* and what your part in it has been. Do you understand?"

There was a pause, then Persoons' voice came through again.

"Yes, Commander," he said. "I'll do what I can to explain, but it's been rough here, and an awful lot has happened. Main thing I want you to understand is that we were forced into this; there was nothing else we could do. If we'd gone on to Hegenis Three, there wouldn't have been any kind of life for us there—the colony was doomed from the start."

"From the beginning, Persoons," Bruce said firmly. "We can't possibly understand if you don't tell us the whole story. And can you send us a picture? Link in your internal cameras, and let me see, as you explain, eh?"

" . . . in the Corps myself, Commander, and you and I, we know about these things . . . Yes, sure, I'll send you a picture . . ."

Lindstrom said softly, "Was he *really* in the Corps do you think?"

"We've had our rotten apples, too, you know," Bruce said, giving her a brief glance. "Just make sure you get everything on tape." Then into the microphone: "Carry on, Persoons; I'm listening."

"What we've done is to bring the ship back to the solar system for justice," Persoons said. "If we'd allowed those bastards to carry on to Hegenis Three . . ."

Alger Morton was a slim, hard-featured man, taut as a wire. His brain was a razor-sharp instrument aimed at the soft underbelly of a commercial empire that ruled a hundred colonial worlds. It was already evaluating this new situation, relating it to stored information and computing what course of action would best serve the interests of Alger Morton. To be head of the Excelsior Corporations Legal Department at the age of thirty-one might have satisfied the ambition of most young men, at least temporarily; but for Alger Morton it was not enough. Nothing was enough.

To Morton, Elkan Niebohr with his benevolent "uncle" image and his folksy humor was the personification of that soft underbelly. He didn't hate Niebohr; his relationship with the human race had long since ceased to include such emotional evaluations. He merely watched the old man, grown soft with easy living, and awaited his opportunity.

"Look, Elkan, one thing for sure," Morton said, leaning forward, with both hands on the President's massive desk as he talked. "With the patrol involved, when that ship gets back to Earth, there's going to be an inquiry."

"We have nothing to hide," Niebohr said. "This is a routine colonization operation."

Morton shrugged. "Things happen, Elkan—little irregularities here, a small omission there. Look, why don't I get my department onto it right away and make sure we've got a clean house, huh?"

"I don't see the necessity for that," Niebohr said cautiously.

"So what's the harm in being prepared?" Morton argued. "If there is anything irregular, those clowns on the CSC are going to take the greatest delight in roasting us over a slow fire."

Niebohr sighed. "All right, Morton, maybe there's

something in what you say. Go ahead with your investigation, and if you do turn up any irregularities, I want to know immediately; understand?"

"Yes, sir." Alger Morton walked out of the President's office, a new spring in his step. The corporation as a whole might be rocked by CSC inquiry, the harder the rocking the better, as long as it was recognized that the man who saved the day was Alger Morton. He began to hum quietly to himself. He had a feeling that he was on his way.

It had been a fantastic performance. The story of the takeover of *Athena* was told. It had been an involved narrative that was at the same time a round trip of the unbelievable convolutions in the mind of Hendrik Persoons. Passing as he talked into a kind of abreaction, there had been times when Persoons screamed, others when he wept, passing from emotion to emotion, as he relived what had happened. There were diatribes of self-justification, whole passages where he screamed his hatred of the oppressive "they" who conspired constantly to rob him of his rights.

But the main burden of his discourse was his rejoicing in the courage and resourcefulness of Hendrik Persoons, the hero who had delivered his people out of the hands of those who intended to maroon them to die on the hellish planet of Hegenis Three. Persoons the orator addressed Bruce, and at the same time the whole solar system, in a manner of such arrogance that he condemned himself out of his own mouth for what he was.

"My God!" Lindstrom said quietly. "The man's completely mad. The way he refused to release the crew—"

Bruce nodded. "He is. You got everything taped?"

"Every inch," Lindstrom said with a shiver.

"How did a potential psychopath like Persoons pass the corporation's exam?" Bruce asked.

Helen said: "Sometimes corporation standards are flexible."

"Then they damned well shouldn't be!" growled Bruce. "Persoons' madness has infected the whole ship."

"But we've got to negotiate with him if we're to save the lives of those people."

"You don't negotiate with a maniac like that; you do as he tells you, or else," Bruce said.

"You're going to save them?"

"I've got to try."

She looked at him sharply. "Is there any doubt? We've handled rescue operations like this before."

Bruce was studying the instruments on the panel ahead of him. "Not quite like this one. In the normal rescue we've been dealing with an already disabled ship; but the *Athena* is still accelerating, and she'll go on doing so until those engines blow out. Matching velocity is going to be quite a problem."

"But we should be able to do it."

"If there's time," Bruce said. "Call control again and see what progress they've made in predicting her course."

Chan came to the door of the President's ward, slid it open and glanced inside at Hurwitz. The surgeon-general looked at him with heavy eyes, and Chan thought, for a moment, that someone ought to order Hurwitz to take some rest. But who?

"The same?" he asked.

"Gradually coming out," said Hurwitz, and kept his eyes on the thin, lightly breathing old figure enveloped in the white of the bed.

Chan came forward. "You do think this is wise?" he asked.

Hurwitz' reply was an aggressive whisper. "The old man is a Christian. Once, when he was young, he wrote hymns, religious songs. This means something to him." He jerked a finger at the door. "Is the priest there?"

"He's outside," Chan said, and his Eastern superiority showed for a second. "Doesn't look a lot like a priest to me."

"Nobody's asking you," Hurwitz said with weary asperity. He walked to the door, and looked out. "Lieutenant Kibbee? Come in, will you?"

A lanky, thin-faced, untidy man, dressed in ill-fitting hospital white, stepped nervously into the room. His red hair was bright as a wreck beacon.

"We're bringing him out of his—sleep—Lieutenant. I understand you know his favorite prayer, don't you?"

Kibbee's voice was quiet and very deep. "Sure, 'God of our world, and of all the other worlds of all time, we call to You . . .' " Kibbee looked anxious. "Is he going to *die*?"

Hurwitz avoided the question; he kept his eyes on the President, who stirred very faintly. The surgeon-general said: "Die? I don't know. But we can't do him any harm, and you might do him some good."

THUNDER OF STARS

In this kind of life,
All things considered,
A spaceman's poor wife
Will tend to get widdered.

(TRADITIONAL JINGLE.)

"WELL, THAT'S one relief, at any rate," Helen Lindstrom said, as the matter-of-fact Cockney voice of PO Dockridge concluded the message. "As far as they can tell, *Athena* isn't likely to hit anything."

Tom Bruce grunted as he visualised *Athena*, like some wild ball, skittering through the already crowded cosmic pool table of the solar system. "Better give 'Clear Space' alert all the same."

"Yes, sir." She called control and gave the message. Then she turned to look at her chief again and found that he was regarding her with a curious half-smile on his lean face.

"You're going to be late on report Friday, Lieutenant Commander," he said. "Maybe I'd better call Admiral Carter and make your apologies, huh?"

"Late?"

Bruce jabbed his finger at the screen, where a blurred blip showed the progress of *Athena*. "The speed she's traveling, we're not going to be able to slow her enough to pull into an orbit round Earth on this swing; maybe not even on the next one."

"Just so long as we do get her in eventually," Helen said. His meaning was obvious to her now. When Scout

Ships Two and Three arrived the operation would still only be in its initial stages. Next would come the tricky task of bringing them sufficiently close to *Athena* so that their magnetic grapples could be engaged onto her hull. Only then, when they were completely secure, would the two scout ships be able to begin using their drives to counteract the tremendous velocity that the colonization ship had built up; and to do so, furthermore, without interfering with her course sufficiently to place her in collision orbit with any other body in the system. Encompassing billions of miles of space, the operation was nevertheless one which was going to demand total accuracy if it were to prove successful.

Admiral Carter and the other members of the Commissioning Board were walking under the great curving underside of *Venturer Twelve*. The monstrous egg was supported by a vast underground system of hydraulic props to accommodate the structural stresses of the ship until the job was finally taken over by her own internal grav system. On the outside skin, red-coveralled welders, using safety harness and magnetic boots, crawled about like flies. At the base, in a great vent where the engine would be fitted, another row of welders, twenty-five meters from the ground, were sealing the engine seatings, being supplied by anti-grav lifts which took up a supply of the arched metal sections. The bright morning air hummed and rattled and sizzled with work.

Carter was just ducking under a safety net when his personal communicator beeped. He pulled it out of his pocket.

"Carter. What is it *now*?"

Pringle's voice managed to sound soothing, even in the buzzy distortion of the little communicator. "Clear space has been ordered, sir."

Her voice was loud enough to be heard by Suvorov, Yow, Mariano and Ericson. The statement brought instant attention.

"What? Who ordered?"

"Lieutenant Commander Bruce sir."

"Bruce—where is he?"

"Command scout—sector RQ364, somewhere out beyond Saturn."

"The hell he is!" exclaimed Carter. "Get onto patrol right away and see what you can find out. I'm coming in."

Trailing the other members of the Commissioning Board like minor satellites, Junius Carter charged across the shipyard to the car park.

Henrik Persoons faced the deputation and roared his contempt. "What the hell did you expect? That it was going to be easy? Maybe you'd rather have gone on to Hegenis Three and rotted there instead of getting back to Earth?"

A small, thin man stepped forward. Ghastly strain was visible on his lined face, his hands shook as he spoke. "We know you've done your best, Hendrik. But this vibration, the screaming of the engines . . . out of phase. Half the children are hysterical and quite a few of the women are beginning to crack up. If they don't get some positive reassurance soon, we're going to have a panic on our hands. There's the crew—engineers—if you—if you release them—"

"They have a right, Hendrik," Kolukwe said nervously as he watched Persoons from close by and recognized the expression. The lips were drawn back from his teeth, the eyes glazed with fury; Persoons had looked like this once before, when he had gone berserk during the battle with the crew. He was deadly dangerous in this state, outside all reason, a man who would stop at nothing.

"Persoons—listen to us!" called a man.

"*Listen*!" hissed Persoons. "You gutless, bloody fools!" Moving with the speed of madness, he lunged across and grabbed at a needle gun that had been lying on a nearby chair. Raising the weapon, he swung it slowly along the line of men who faced him.

"Now *you* listen to me," he snarled. "Get off this bridge before I stitch the whole damned lot of you!"

Persoons was not watching Kolukwe, taking it for granted that Joe would support any move he made. But there had already been too many deaths. Joe launched himself forward, bringing the edge of his big hand down in a chop to the side of Persoons' neck. The Eurasian slumped to the deck, the needle gun dropping with a clatter from his nerveless fingers.

Joe Kolukwe, kneeling beside Persoons, looked up at them. He said: "Hendrik Persoons is dead." Then he shouted: "The crew—down there! If we let them out—"

At that moment the deck beneath their feet lurched and heaved, as a massive, rumbling explosion coursed through the *Athena*. For about thirty seconds it was as though the big ship had been grasped in the jaws of some gigantic animal which was intent on shaking the life out of it.

And then the sound and the fury were gone; the angry roaring of the opposing engines was silenced at last, and men began to struggle to their feet. The only noises now were the humming of the air conditioning and the electronic equipment—and something else; it was a *nothing*, a negation of sound, and Joe Kolukwe finally recognized it as the silence between the stars.

He shivered. "That's it," he said. "The Grenbachs have blown. I'd better talk to Commander Bruce. The rest of you, get Persoons out of here, then go back and do what you can for the others. Tell them everything is under control, that all we have to do is wait, and keep calm. Now, the engineers! We'll let them out!"

Tom Bruce nodded as he spoke to the dark, solemn face in the vidscreen. "Scouts Two and Three should join us within the next hour. After that, it's just a matter of getting them into position, then we can begin to do something about slowing you down."

"Thank you, Commander," Joe Kolukwe said. "We're all mighty grateful for what you're doing."

"Well, *don't* be," Bruce said harshly. "When we get you back to Earth, my guess is that you're going to wish we'd just let you go on into interstellar space. They'll crucify you, and anyone who took part in this mutiny."

"I realize that, sir," Joe Kolukwe said humbly. "But at least the women and the kiddies will be saved. Maybe that will make it all worthwhile. And if the radiation leaks hadn't killed the crewmen, we . . ."

Tom Bruce fought back the sympathy that welled into his mind for this gentle, unassuming man. This was no time for pity. Coupling mutiny with murder, they had now placed themselves in a position where the valuable lives of loyal members of the Space Corps would have to be risked in order to save them from the consequences of their criminal folly.

"Yes—Persoons' death?"

"It was necessary sir. There are eight witnesses." Kolukwe's eyes lowered.

"I'm not *blaming* you, man," Bruce said. "Pity someone didn't do the job sooner; Persoons was a maniac. Then the crew would have been saved."

"He was doing what he believed in," Kolukwe said.

Bruce grunted and changed the subject. "Kolukwe, I'm going to be quite frank with you. Your main job is going to be that of keeping your people aboard there from panicking. They'll be in free-fall conditions for quite a long time, and there may be some rough moments."

"We understand that, sir," said Joe Kolukwe.

"Good!" Bruce said. "Link your transmitter with the internal scanners aboard the ship so that we can get some idea of what's going on there."

"I'll do what I can, Commander," Kolukwe said.

"We don't expect miracles." Bruce switched off his microphone and turned to his second in command. "Well?"

Helen Lindstrom's face was very pale. "Moon and Mars operators agree with me," she said. "When the drive exploded it changed *Athena*'s course—slightly."

"Slightly? How the hell much is that?" Bruce demanded with sudden savagery.

"We're working on it now," Helen said. "But it doesn't look good."

"Let me know as soon as you've got anything definite," Bruce said. Turning his attention back to his own communications set, he began to talk to Scout Ships Two and Three.

THUNDER OF STARS

Never forget that Man in space is an intruder, vulnerable at all times, faced by immeasurable hostile odds, entirely dependent on the maintenance of the artificial environment of the ship in which he travels.

(MANUAL FOR SPACE
CORPS OFFICERS.
P 167. Revised Ed. 2160)

IF HELEN Lindstrom had not been tough she would never have reached her present rank, but as she listened to the operators on Moon and Mars arguing, she found her eyes smarting with suppressed tears, not because of the colorful language of the operators, but because she was watching the screen that showed the transmission from *Athena*. The picture changed every ten seconds, as it automatically switched from one internal scanner to the next, a procedure originally intended to give a captain on his bridge a composite picture of what was going on all over his ship. As it changed, faces appeared, suddenly individualized—men, women, children, gray with tension, their eyes haunted by fear of the unknown and knowledge of their own helplessness. She tried to force herself to look elsewhere, but always her eyes swung back, however unwillingly.

Moon and Mars argued, matched figures, and argued again. And as she listened to them, Helen Lindstrom was forced closer and closer to the conclusion that she was trying to avoid. She was the observer on the spot, and the data she got from the command scout, out there in space, was more accurate than anything that could be seen from any planetary tracking station. In the end, the casting vote in the matter of determining *Athena*'s new course vector must be hers.

Turning her head so that the vid screen was out of sight, she made an attempt to close up on all emotion, to think herself into the course-and-speed computer. She wanted to be nothing but part of the machine, part of the complex that supplied Tom Bruce with operational information. At the same time she consoled herself with the thought that, however difficult her task might seem, she was still only the penultimate arbiter. The decision about what action should be taken on the data she provided would be his. It was a dreadful responsibility.

She fought against recognizing the truth as the figures flashed up on the screen of the computer, canceled out and began again, using her own data. Hoping against hope that the Mars operator had made some error, that the conclusions of the Moon observers were nearer the truth. But Moon was in a bad position, the angle and distance were both against the likelihood of their being correct.

The results came up, confirming Mars so closely as to leave no doubt in her mind.

"How long?" asked Tom Bruce.

She turned to face him gratefully. He already knew this terrible thing that she could not put into words.

"Approximately six hours. Oh, God, Tom!" She felt the hysteria closing in on her mind as she imagined what it must be like aboard *Athena*. She found herself struggling with her safety harness, tearing at the straps.

"Lindstrom!" Bruce's voice was like a whiplash, cutting through her confusion.

"Sir!"

"Call Scout Ships Two and Three and tell them to return to base. There's nothing for them to do here now."

World Admiral Joe Hoffner was still waiting in the anteroom. He looked up as the surgeon-general entered.

"Well?"

"It will take all the skill we've got," Hurwitz said. "Also a bit of luck, and a couple more prayers wouldn't hurt. Perhaps the old chap doesn't *want* to live any more. Perhaps we are the ones who are forcing him."

Hoffner was aghast. "But he must! Look at all he's got to live for. The way he cares about people, and the way people care about *him*!"

Hurwitz shook his head somberly. "It's sort of crept up on him as he's got older. He's been shielded more and more, smothered with love and care. Once, when he was younger, he had raw decisions to make. He was part of life, of the whole business of Earth, the solar system and the colonies beyond. But he's loved more now as—as a museum piece—by many people . . ."

Hoffner strode the length of the silent carpet and came back. "What do I tell the news services?"

"Nothing."

Hoffner swung his arms helplessly. "All right. If you say so."

A knock at the door. An orderly entered, carrying a portable vidphone set.

"Yes?"

"May I plug this in, sir?"

Hurwitz stabbed a finger at the wallplug. "If you must. Who wants to talk? We're busy."

"Lieutenant Commander Bruce, System Patrols, sir."

"*Bruce*?" Hurwitz looked wonderingly at Hoffner. "All right, leave it," he said to the orderly. Bending over the set, he switched it on. The picture shivered, then steadied.

"Yes, Commander?" Huwritz said.

"Sir, I must speak to the President," Bruce said.

"Impossible!"

"That's what I was told, sir. And that's why I'm calling *you*. It's absolutely essential that I speak with the President personally."

"Fong?"

"No, sir. This isn't a political matter."

"World Admiral Hoffner is right here with me," Hurwitz said.

"It's no good, sir," Bruce insisted. "Even he can't give me permission for this."

Hoffner put his head by the side of Hurwitz. "Permission for *what*?"

Bruce's face was a duty mask, his voice was flat, as though all feeling had been ironed out of it by sheer will power. "I may have to kill five hundred people," he said.

The picture transmission from *Athena* could have been a schoolroom or a mission hall somewhere, anywhere. A couple of dozen children sat, listening to a young woman in gray coveralls who was reading to them from the Holy Bible. The woman's voice was steady and clear, but her hands, holding the book, were shaking.

Lindstrom rounded desperately on Bruce. "Do we have to have that foul thing on?' she demanded. "Won't the recording be enough—without our seeing it?"

Bruce glanced at her. "All right, cut the picture for the time being. Maybe it's best that we don't see ... *everything*."

"Tom ... there *has* to be some other way." She heard her own voice, like a moan of pain.

Bruce said harshly: "In just sixty-five minutes from now that ship is going to hit Earth."

"I ... I could be wrong. Tom! If I were wrong."

"There's no *if*!" His voice crackled. "We're the only ones in a position to stop *Athena*."

Her lips trembled. "Five hundred people," she said.

"Against *how* many?" he said. "Look on it as a mathematical problem—just *try*. Even if that thing hits Earth in the middle of the Pacific—"

She shook her head. "No ... not the Pacific. Northeastern United States—New York conurbation."

"Christ Almighty!" Bruce said. He closed his eyes momentarily.

"Commander Bruce . . . Commander Bruce . . . *Athena* calling Commander Bruce," said a loudspeaker.

"Picture!" he ordered sharply.

Helen Lindstrom touched the switch and the face of Joe Kolukwe appeared on the screen.

"Yes, Kolukwe?" Tom Bruce said.

"Commander, I know you've got a lot to do," Kolukwe said apologetically. "But some of our people back there are mighty nervous—you see, they don't understand what's going on. I've tried to explain to them, but, well ... I'm just a simple cloddie myself. I was wondering if maybe I could switch into the PA system and you could talk to them for just a minute or two."

"Oh, *God*!" she whispered.

Bruce flashed her a brief glance, then turned back to the scanner. "I read you, Kolukwe. But right now I'm tied. There's a great deal that has to be done."

"Just a few words ... a bit of reassurance, Commander," Joe Kolukwe said. "That's all they need ... that, and to see your face, and know there's somebody out there who cares what happens to them."

Helen looked at Bruce's bony face, weirdly lit from below. Near the left temple she could see the quick throbbing of a vein. Then she looked down at the missile board where two red lights were already glowing.

"All right, Tom, I'll talk to them," she said. "You do what you have to do."

"Thanks, Helen." He flashed her a quick smile, and for a moment they were close again, a man and a woman sharing—duty, love ... Here, in this inhuman situation, there was some consolation in remembering one's humanity.

"Hallo, Joe Kolukwe," she said, smiling into the scanner. "My name is Helen Lindstrom, and I'm Commander Bruce's number two. If you'll put me on your internal PA screens maybe I can explain things to your people. You see, what we're going to do is bring in ..."

Tom Bruce flipped the switch that armed the already lowered missiles. Now it was only a matter of lining up the two silver circles of the aiming mechanism. In the background he could hear Helen Lindstrom's voice, cool and efficient, as she explained the procedure for ferrying a crippled ship into orbit. *But not this ship*, he thought grimly, his hand locking ship control and aiming device together.

Now the silver circles impinged. Time stretched and stretched and stretched.

He thought, *She has a beautiful voice.*

The circles merged, became one. Bruce's hand was on the firing stud.

" ... very often find that with a few simple repairs a

ship . . ." Helen Lindstrom's voice, calm, reassuring. The statue face of Joe Kolukwe in the vidscreen was joined by another now, an African woman, who must be his wife.

Tom Bruce pressed the firing buttons. Came two thudding kicks as the missiles launched; he began to swing the scout ship into a turn.

He became aware that Helen had stopped talking. She was staring silently at the faces of the two people in the screen.

And they, in their turn, were staring back at her, the beginnings of real fear, of uncertainty, clouding their faces.

"All right, that's enough!" Bruce snapped. Leaning across, he switched off the transmitter.

Helen made no response. She sat rigid, staring at the blank screen.

Bruce was watching the picture from the exterior scanners. It showed *Athena*, faintly glowing, set against a frame of starshot blackness.

Two needles of fire threaded their way across the screen. They touched the ship. For a tiny moment, nothing happened. Then, a great orange, purple-edged flower of flame blossomed out, silent, horrible, total, final.

The flower wilted, disintegrated into a billion fading particles. Soon, only the stars remained.

THUNDER OF STARS

It's wonderful how your beauty grows,
When you're three months out in space,
And handsome become the most ordinary Joes,
Apollos in figure and face. . . .

(SONG OF THE CREWWOMEN).

HELEN LINDSTROM blinked as the sunlight glared on the vast, mirror-polished egg of *Venturer Twelve*. Noticing that her companions on the antigrav lift, Admiral Carter and Chief Petty Officer Panos, had slipped on the dark goggles that came with the protective clothing the three of them were wearing, she followed suit, grateful as much for the masking effect they had on her features as for the protection they afforded against glare. Here in the shipyard, in the middle of his own cabbage patch, Admiral Junius Carter was as tractable as a well-fed bulldog, clearly pleased with himself and what he was doing, and enjoying the task of showing the newly appointed 2 i/c and warrant officer over the ship. But she still found herself wary of the man, and unable to forget the hard time he had given her during the Commissioning Board interview.

"Well, what do you think of her?"

Helen came out of her private thoughts and became aware that Admiral Carter, squat and slightly clownlike in his red-and-white-striped coveralls, and a bright red helmet with two stars of rank, was addressing her. "Magnificent, sir," she said.

"You're damned right she is!" Carter said, grinning. "The biggest and the best!"

Panos, a dark, Mediterranean type in early middle age, built like a barrel, nodded his agreement. She liked what she had seen of this swarthy-faced man. He was undemonstrative, but filled with a restrained enthusiasm, and she had a feeling that she would be able to work well with him.

The a/g lift hovered in midair, about six meters from the outermost bulge of the ship's skin. Standing at its edge, near the safety rail, they watched the welders, moving about the hull.

"That silly sod thinks he's walking on air—look at him!" barked Carter, as one of the steelmen, negotiating a piece of scaffolding, swung over backward. The man made a kicking motion, attempting to engage both his magnetic boots, and missed. There was a yell, and he fell some twenty meters before his safety line brought him up with a wrench that must have come close to unsocketing his arms. He dangled some distance from them, wriggling like an angry marionette as he was pulled up toward the jury-rigged platform on top of the hull.

Carter looked upward. "Foran's up there. You met him yet?"

"No, sir," said Panos. "But I've heard about him."

"Great feller!" Carter said. "You'll either like him or want to fight him on sight, but he's the best foreman in the business." He turned, and told the driver to take them up.

The a/g lift bucked and weaved as it climbed the air currents. The platform on top of the hull was built partly across the great gap which would eventually house the control and bridge area of the ship. Looking down, Helen caught her breath as she saw clear through the center of the massive structure to the ground beneath, where distant men scurried about like ants. She hung onto the safety rail as the lift fought against gusty winds, feeling the joints of her fingers cracking. Finally the driver managed to settle his craft and lock it onto the metal plate set into the platform for that purpose.

Foran came to meet them. He was about one meter eighty five, big built and gray haired, with a face like tanned leather, and bright blue eyes.

"Afternoon, Admiral."

"Afternoon, Dan. Meet Lieutenant Commander Lindstrom and Chief Petty Officer Panos."

They shook hands.

"Give me a minute, will you, Admiral?" said Foran, as the steelman who had lost his footing was hauled to the top. Foran strode across the platform, his face grim set.

"Let's see your boots, Poliakov."

"I'm okay."

"Show me your boots!" roared Foran.

The steelman complied meekly. Foran took the battery out of the big square toe of the boot and held it up for inspection.

"Just as I thought—yesterday's date!" bawled Foran. "You're fined a day's pay, Poliakov. Now get to hell out of here and draw yourself a new set; git!"

Dan Foran was not a man with whom you argued, in this or any other mood. Poliakov picked up his boots and high-tailed it for the temporary lift, which ran by the hoist down through the hole in the center of the hull. Foran watched him go, then walked back to join Helen and her two companions.

"They never change," he said, with a big grin. "They're on piece work, so they won't even use time to make sure that their boots'll hold 'em. Just take a chance on the safety harness. Got steelmen here who take home as much a week as a Lieutenant Commander. Now, Admiral; anything particular on your mind, or is this just a general look-see?"

Carter was flipping through the pages of a large notebook. "I'm a bit behind with my homework. It's been a busy two days."

"Yeah, I figured it had been." Foran looked sympathetic. "That inquiry is going to be a big circus."

Carter nodded gloomily.

"I sure hope Bruce comes out of it okay," Foran said. "Like you said last week, he's the only man for the job. But if they tie a can to his tail . . ." he pursed his lips seriously.

Helen stiffened at the sound of the name, but said nothing.

"The whole Corps is behind him," Carter said, with a sudden gruffness. "Now, Dan, about the housing of the bridge section—I'd like you to have a look at these stress figures." He and Foran walked away across the platform, deeply immersed in a highly technical discussion, and Helen was left alone with CPO Panos.

"Is the Admiral really in favor of Tom Bruce for command of *Venturer Twelve*?" she asked.

Panos shrugged his heavy shoulders. "There have been rumors. It would suit me. He's a fine officer."

Helen eyed the CPO sharply, but there was no sign of anything other than sincerity on his round, swarthy face. "You know him?" she asked.

"I was with him on *Venturer Ten*," Panos explained. "He was a Lieutenant then, but you could tell he had the stuff in him. Even then he was a man who didn't hesitate to make a difficult decision, whatever the consequences to himself. That time down on Minos IV, plenty of officers would have . . ." Panos stopped talking suddenly, his face going a shade darker. "Sorry, Commander, I'm afraid I'm talking too much."

"No, Panos, go on," Helen said. "I'd like to hear."

Panos looked down at his feet, and shuffled slightly. "Better not, if its all the same to you. The Admiral would have my balls if he caught me talking about it."

Helen made no attempt to restrain her smile. "All right, Panos; some other time, eh? Now, what shall we talk about—the view? Or maybe you'd like to give me some of your preliminary thoughts on the matter of crew discipline?"

"The way it looks to me, we shouldn't hit any difficulty there," Panos said seriously. "Med/Psyche have done a first-class selection job. We shall be getting nothing but the cream."

"Glad to hear it," Helen said. "Although, if they're that good, they're going to take some living up to."

"Two years second in command to Tom Bruce, you shouldn't have any trouble," Panos said.

"Thanks for the kind words, Panos." Helen spoke with deliberate lightness, but her own reservations still remained.

She could not rid herself of the feeling that she was like some amputated limb, no longer part of the larger organism, and yet without the self-sufficiency required to carry on an independent existence.

Carter's discussion with Foran was concluded. He trundled back toward them and said: "Right; we'll take the hoist lift down. I want to see how Commander Baker is getting along with the drive installations."

As the creaking, swaying lift made its way through the center of the massive hull, it was like going down past the various levels of some half-completed, highly technical hell. Thick cables led off in all directions like great serpents, and men in brightly colored coveralls crawled, swung and crouched everywhere like attendant demons. The whole was lit by the flashing of welding torches, and sound effects were provided by the clanging, whining cacophony of metal being trimmed and shaped. The sound seemed amplified by the rounded shape of the hull, bouncing from one surface to another and smashing in on the human ear with a daemonic ferocity that caused Helen and her companions to don the earmuffs that were part of their protective clothing.

Finally the lift slanted down away from the engine area and passed out of the bottom of the hull through a smaller vent into a clearing in the forest of hydraulic jacks. The activity in this area was no less intense, but the noise at least was slightly more bearable. Reaching ground level, the lift stopped with a bump and the party stepped off onto the fused rock floor, and into a bewildering metropolis of trucks, handling machinery and piles of dumped material.

"There's Commander Baker," said Carter.

Ten meters away from them, a long-limbed officer in blue coveralls stood with his back to them, bawling instructions through a loud-hailer. He was looking upward, toward a team of men who were having some difficulty in maneuvering a huge, cone-shaped piece of metal which Helen recognized as an auxiliary drive jet.

As she followed Carter across the floor, Helen reflected that seldom in her service career had she heard such a colorful and inventive stream of profanity as that being pumped out of the loud-hailer in the direction of the struggling engineers.

"Afternoon, Baker, how's it going?" asked Carter, as they reached the officer.

Commander Baker lowered the loud-hailer and turned to face them. "Going? This palsied lot of ruptured eunuchs? Got their tiny brains in their arses! But we'll manage somehow, I guess."

Admiral Carter nodded. "You usually do. Now, if you can spare a moment, I'd like you to meet Lieutenant Commander Lindstrom and CPO Panos—the Second in Command and Warrant Officer of this tub. Panos puts up his new rank at the end of the week."

Commander Baker turned to look at Helen and her companion. "Glad to know you, Commander." Baker shook hands heartily.

"Commander Baker," acknowledged Helen, looking up at the broom-handle figure and hard-bitten features of the tall officer. There was little doubt that Commander Baker had seen all kinds of service, and he must now be over the age when regulations demanded that he should be grounded.

"Nick Panos," Baker said, moving forward and thrusting out a gloved hand toward the CPO. "Long time no see!"

"Commander." CPO Panos' face darkened slightly as he shook hands with the officer. "Glad to see you again."

Baker turned to Helen, baring discolored teeth in a death's head grin. "Finest bloody PO in the Corps, you've got here, Commander. Glad you're making warrant rank, Nick."

Helen watched the engineer closely. There was something about Baker, something that she was unable to define, that left her with a feeling of uneasiness.

"Fine!" Baker said, punching Panos in his ample middle. He turned to Carter. "I wanted to have a word with you and Chalovsky about these damned auxiliary jets—they're hell to install, and they're not going to be much better when it comes to any servicing. If we could allow slightly more space . . ."

"Why don't we go up and take a look?" Carter said.

"Yes, that would be best." Commander Baker and the Admiral walked across to a small a/g lift and began to float up toward the party of engineers, who were still struggling with the jet.

"The Admiral will never make grade A as a tourist guide, will he?" Helen said, with a grin as she and Panos watched them go. "Maybe it would have been best if he'd let us mooch around and find our own way about."

"What, and miss the pleasure of showing off his baby?" Panos said.

They dodged to one side to avoid a hooting lift truck.

"You've served with just about everybody, seems to me," Helen said. "Where did you know Commander Baker from?"

"She was an engineer on *Venturer Eight*," Panos said.

Helen gaped. "She?"

"Why, sure—First Lieutenant Sarah Baker she was then," Panos said.

Helen stared up at the a/g lift, at the angular, sexless figure that towered a good six inches above the squat form of Admiral Carter.

"My God!" she murmured, unable to restrain a shudder.

"Commander?" said the CPO, his head slightly to one side, questioning.

"Nothing, Panos, *nothing*," she said briskly.

Back in her quarters, Helen Lindstrom peeled off her clinging uniform and headed thankfully for the shower. It had been a long, energy-sapping day. Afterward, dried, powdered and perfumed, she put on a robe and walked through into the sitting room.

Corps officers' quarters at the shipyard were comfortable, if not luxurious. In the sitting room there was a multi-channel TV, an automatic-selection stereo tape player, a vidphone and a small bar. Air conditioned and insulated against the intrusion of any extraneous noise, it was a place where an officer could enjoy complete privacy during off-duty hours—a luxury that was hardly possible during service in space—and it was thus all the more appreciated.

With the stereo playing quietly, she poured herself a glass of fine sherry and sat down, attempting by self-imposed calmness to quell her twitching muscles and raw nerve endings. The music was ancient, although the recording was modern—Harold Greenberg playing the Bach Partita in E Major. Normally she found the clean, weaving lines of the single violin soothing in their logical progression, but this evening the magic failed to work.

Rising impatiently, she strode across and switched off the tape player.

Exasperated further by her own lack of inner resource, she switched on the TV. She found a news magazine program. A silver-haired, young-faced commentator, wearing old-fashioned, dark rimmed glasses, was speaking.

". . . the Court of Inquiry into the *Athena* colonization ship disaster, which begins on Tuesday in Lake Cities, with Supreme Court Judge Alote Jones presiding."

Helen leaned forward, her attention caught at last, as the commentator continued.

"Still on the subject of the *Athena* disaster, head of the Excelsior Corporation Legal Department, Alger Morton, held a news conference which was attended by representatives from all media."

The studio scene dissolved, to be replaced by a head and shoulders shot of a thin-faced man with slicked-down, dark hair. Helen shuddered at the coldness of the eyes and the uncompromising mouth.

"We at Excelsior welcome a full and unrestricted inquiry into all the circumstances leading to the *Athena* disaster. We are fully aware of our public duty and we have nothing to hide.

"Aspersions have already been cast on the character of Captain Lacombe. I would remind you that Captain Lacombe is no longer able to defend himself, but we are prepared to produce sworn testimony of the highest authority that in all his years of service, Captain Lacombe never swerved from loyalty and devotion to his task as an interstellar ship commander. Excelsior will accept no gag nor any white-washing. We stand for humanity and freedom, the freedom to speak the truth . . ."

Helen clenched her fists as she stared at the narrow face on the screen.

Morton continued: "We shall produce expert testimony to prove that there is considerable doubt as to whether the *Athena*, if allowed to continue on the course she was following at the time of her destruction, would indeed have come within a million miles of Earth! If this is the case, then logically it must follow that the lives of these poor people were sacrificed needlessly, sacrificed by a quasi-military organization that hides its incompetence under a cloak of security. Security against what? Could it be against the truth?"

The pinched face of the lawyer faded from the screen, to be replaced by that of the commentator.

"Mr. Morton, the head of Excelsior Corporation's Legal Department was speaking at a press conference earlier today. With tension rising, the Court of Inquiry promises to be the biggest legal event of the year."

She switched off the TV. On Tuesday her career, her relationship with Tom Bruce, would be placed ruthlessly on the public dissection table.

She walked across to the vidphone and switched it on.

"Get me Commander Bruce, at System Patrol HQ."

The picture fuzzed into an abstract pattern, then a few seconds later re-formed into a human face. But it was not the face she had hoped to see.

"Good evening, Commander," PO Dockridge said cheerfully. "I'm afraid Commander Bruce isn't here at present. He and Lieutenant Takaki are putting the command ship through her paces."

"I . . . see," Helen said, unable to hide her disappointment.

"He should be back in a couple of hours," Dockridge said helpfully. "Would you like me to give him a message?"

"No, Dockridge, no message. Don't tell him I called. It's not important."

Dockridge's face lost some of its jauntiness. "Is everything all right, Commander?" he asked.

She felt a sudden surge of nostalgia for the familiar surroundings of System Patrol, for the people she had known and worked with for so long.

"Thank you, Dockridge. Good night," she said sharply and switched off the vidphone. The quiet of the room began to close in on her again. Flinging off the robe, she started to dress.

Twenty minutes later she was seated on a high stool against the bar counter in the officers' mess. She was beginning to realize that she was just as much alone here as she had been in the privacy of her quarters. The number-two uniform had been a mistake too; this was mainly a transit mess, and nobody seemed to be wearing anything more formal than number threes. Some were even in civilian clothes. She sat, staring moodily into an ice-frosted glass of apéritif, still feeling out of place.

She had almost decided to empty her glass and retreat back to her quarters without going through the prolonged ordeal of eating alone, when a hoarse voice spoke at her elbow.

"Hello there, Commander. Mind if I join you?"

She turned her head and found herself looking up into the lined, weather-beaten face of Commander Sarah Baker. Baker was wearing a dog-eared, rather faded suit of number threes. Her short-cut, grayish hair was neatly brushed, and in a cursory gesture of femininity she had outlined her thin lips with deep red lipstick. In combination with her irregular, brownish teeth, the effect was not entirely successful, Helen decided. And then, suffering a sudden attack of conscience about having such bitchy thoughts, she returned Baker's smile with warmth.

"Of course. What will you have?"

Baker, almost predictably, called for bourbon on the rocks, which she drank quickly, at one swallow.

"Ah! That's better," she said, thrusting the glass across the counter. The steward was ready with an immediate refill, as if used to this evening ritual. "After a day out there, a couple of drinks are the only thing that can bring you back to feeling like a human being again."

"That's quite a job you're doing, Commander," Helen said. "I can understand that it must be a strain; the noise alone would fray my edges."

"Hell! You get used to it." Baker tackled her second drink with the same speed, and Helen found herself wondering just how long she sustained this pace. "The name's Sarah, by the way. What's yours?"

"Helen."

Baker's gray eyes swept appraisingly over Helen's immaculate figure. "Good! Suits you. Have another drink, Helen."

The look left Helen with a curiously uneasy feeling, but not wishing to appear unsociable, she agreed.

This time Baker took only a mouthful of her whisky and replaced her glass on the counter. "Smoke?" she said, producing a packet of dark, thin cigars.

Helen shook her head. "No thanks, I don't." The cigars, she noted, were the same brand that Tom Bruce smoked.

"Good for you; filthy habit," Baker said, lighting up. "Well, what did you think of *Twelve*?"

"She's going to be a fine ship."

"The best," Baker said, her lined face wreathed in blue smoke. "I envy you, going out in her."

"Panos was telling me you were in *Venturer Eight*."

Baker grimaced. "Yes, and I haven't been off this damned planet since. Med/Psyche grounded me for some stupid reason."

"I'm sorry."

"Comes to all of us in the end," Baker said. "Look at old Junius—he'd give his testicles to be back out there in the big blue, but instead he has to make do with building ships for people who can. Still, it's better than early retirement; *that*'s the real killer."

Helen felt a surge of sympathy for this hard-bitten, slightly grotesque woman, with her mannish figure and life-battered face. After perhaps twenty years of devotion to her chosen profession, after giving the most meaningful part of her life, she was, in effect, on the scrapheap. Other women of her age had husbands, children and grandchildren, but for someone like Sarah Baker there was nothing to look forward to but a useless, lonely retirement. Life, the normal life of a woman, was something that women like Baker never had the chance to experience. *Women like Baker*; Helen realized with a stab of pain that what she was really thinking was *women like me*.

"Panos was telling me you had trouble with *Venturer*

Eight," Helen said, making a desperate effort to keep her tone conversational.

"Uh-uh. She was a bitch." Baker downed her drink and ordered another. "They spent eighteen months trying to iron out the bugs in her steering system. They got it right, and then the first time we got out beyond Mars the whole damned shoot junked again and we had to call for help."

Helen listened, personal heart-searchings forgotten as Baker talked of the voyage of *Venturer Eight*. Plunging back into memory, the strange bony features of the woman took on a new life, seeming to bring back the image of the younger, less hard-bitten female creature who had once inhabited that gaunt frame.

Some twenty minutes later, even though she had drunk only three glasses against Baker's half-dozen or more, Helen was beginning to feel a certain headiness, and to have difficulty in focusing her eyes properly. "Phew!" she exclaimed, grasping the edge of the counter as a sudden dizziness hit her.

"What's the matter?" asked Baker.

"Stupid of me," Helen said. "I'm not much of a drinker, and I didn't have any lunch."

"You poor kid!" Baker said, putting one strong brown hand on Helen's arm. "Here am I blowing off like this, and you're starving."

"Not really," Helen said. "But I suppose I ought to eat something."

"In that case, why don't we go along to my quarters?" Baker said. "I could fix you up with a snack, an omelet maybe?"

"Very kind of you," Helen said. In her present state she was quite prepared to have her decisions made for her.

"The food in this mausoleum is only fit for spacemen and horses anyway," Baker said, grinning. "You'll be far better off with my cooking." Slipping her arm through Helen's, she helped her down from the stool. The two of them walked out of the officers' mess together.

Baker's quarters were the exact duplicate of those Helen herself was occupying; the same pastel-colored walls, carpets and built-in amenities. Despite the fact that Baker must have occupied these rooms for some time, and would most probably do so for some time to come, the only mark of individuality was a large painting which hung on the wall at right angles to the TV screen.

Seated alone on the sofa, while Sarah Baker played host at the bar, Helen's eyes were drawn irresistibly to the painting. Executed in curiously shimmering oils, its subject was a slim, dark-haired girl of considerable beauty. The girl was wearing a long pink dress of some semi-transparent material, possibly chiffon, and she was dancing. Captured in this frozen moment, the artist had somehow managed to convey at the same time a dynamic impression of movement. Against the background of a starry night sky, the girl danced eternally, with her arms outstretched, her eyes looking toward something, or somebody, who was out of sight beyond the border of the canvas.

"How beautiful!" Helen said, completely captivated by the portrait.

"Romantic twaddle!" Sarah Baker said gruffly, thrusting an ice-tinkling glass into Helen's hand. "I call it 'Star Dancer.' "

"*You* painted it?" Helen said, looking up into the lined features.

Sarah Baker nodded. "Used to do quite a lot at one time. Made a change from bloody engine rooms and the stink of grease." She sat down beside Helen.

"I'm not much of a judge, but I think it's very good," Helen said sincerely. It crossed her mind that the painting was in some strange way a self-portrait of Sarah Baker, not as she ever was, but as she might have been, in her dreams, many years before. As she realized this, Helen felt a bond of sympathy with Baker stronger than anything that had gone before. This woman had experienced all the conflicts, all the misgivings about herself as a woman and at the same time a Corps officer, that Helen had been going through. In an unconscious expression of this rare moment of understanding, Helen reached out and touched Sarah Baker's hand, holding it with a gentle firmness.

Baker's response was immediate and shattering. Helen fought to free herself from the grasp of those wiry arms, whimpering in terror as she realized just how disastrously misjudged her gesture of sympathy had been. The struggle was brief. Baker was probably more than a match for Helen physically. Certainly in the first moments of the struggle she had the advantage; but when their faces came close together, and she recognized the disgust and loathing in Helen's eyes, the heart went out of her. Releasing her grip, she turned her back on Helen and slumped into the corner of the sofa, head in her hands.

Shivering with shock and horror, Helen stood up and rearranged her uniform. Then, without a word, she bolted from the room, slamming the door behind her.

Her own quarters were mercifully near. She opened the door with trembling hands and staggered through into the bathroom, where she retched up the acid contents of her stomach. Afterward, she stood shivering, regarding her streaming eyes and smeared face in the mirror and cursing herself for being such a stupid, naïve fool.

The entire humiliating episode had been her fault.

She should have realized what Baker was from the first, and for herself, apparently, to make the first physical move was unforgivable. But it had seemed at the time that Baker and she had so much in common, that they had suffered from the same kind of problems and could help each other.

What she had not realized was the fact that Baker, over the long, hard years, had found an answer that fitted in with her own, personal mental makeup: women in a man's universe either capitulated or became men themselves.

"She's one hell of a ship, Commander, that's for sure," said PO Nick Panos. He pitched his gravelly voice high to cut through the echoing clangor of noise.

They were standing on a temporary flooring laid over girders, below which could be seen the huge, bow-like curve of the engine area. In the center was the forty meter circular vent, round which steelmen squatted, working on the arcs of lining which an anti-gravity lift was ferrying up to them from the ground below. Helen Lindstrom nodded. She was looking down through the vent at a foreshortened figure in blue coveralls which stood, loud-hailer to mouth, bawling instructions to men working above.

She and Panos were conducting their own tour of inspection. They had arranged this between themselves as a way of getting to know the ship, and the members of the crew who were already working on her, supervising the installation of equipment relating to their specialty. Without the forbidding presence of Admiral Carter, they found themselves accepted with a lesser degree of formality, and Helen would have enjoyed herself had it not been for her continual awareness of Commander Sarah Baker down there on the floor beneath the engines vent.

"That looks like Lieutenant Maranne, the radar officer," Panos said, squinting upward, as a trim figure stepped off the hoist lift at a level some thirty meters above them. "Shall we go up and have a word with her?"

Helen made a sudden decision. "You go on up, Panos," she said. "I want to see those heavy-grade engine liners that Chalovsky was talking about."

"I'll come with you, then," Panos said immediately.

"No!" Helen was aware that even against the background of noise, her voice was suddenly strident. "Go ahead, Panos, I'll join you in the Radar section later."

Panos looked at her curiously, then shrugged. "All right, Commander." He turned and walked toward the spot where the descending hoist lift would come to rest.

Helen watched his broad back for a moment, then walked hurriedly in the other direction. Grabbing a rope, she lowered herself down onto the engine floor, not far from where the whining, spitting welders were working on the rim. A safety officer would have disapproved of her method of transit. She walked toward them and looked down.

Sarah Baker was still there. The loud-hailer was tucked under her arm now, as she stood talking to the driver of a truck that had just come up with a fresh load of metal for the engine linings. GD men were taking the sections from the truck and piling them onto an anti-grav lift.

"Not too close, please, Commander," said a voice at Helen's elbow.

She turned, to find herself face to face with a small man in the bright yellow fluorescent coverall suit of a safety officer. "Good morning; Mr. Cohen, isn't it?"

The man nodded, evidently pleased at her recognition after only a brief introduction on the previous day.

"That's right, Commander. Don't mind my interference—that's my job."

"Of course," Helen said.

"The Admiral's the worst," Cohen said. "Three, four times a week I have to pull him up over something or other. He just doesn't seem to give a damn."

Helen grinned. "A fair description of Junius Carter's philosophy." She wondered if Cohen had seen her come down.

"He's a great man," Cohen said, nodding his head. "With a man like—" He stopped, suddenly alert, his eyes staring beyond her.

Helen turned to see the underside of a loaded anti-grav lift which had just come up through the vent.

As she watched, a wisp of smoke came from the side of the lift.

"His coils are burning!" shouted Cohen. "Damned fools! I've told them time and again about overloading." He ran toward the edge of the vent, looking upward and blowing his whistle. Several welders stopped working and looked up.

The lift was lowering now, bucking and swaying as it moved, still out in the center of the vent. More smoke came from its side, then a spark, then a shower. The driver's face was a pale, frightened blur; his mouth was open.

"Don't try to get it up here!" Cohen called. "You won't have the power. Take it *down* while you still have some left!"

The driver made no response. Only his fear-ridden eyes moved. He stood paralyzed by the recognition that one touch on the controls could mean instant failure of the coils. The lift bucked, emitting another shower of sparks.

Helen was at the edge of the rim; Cohen was too busy to even notice her. Down below the vent, on the ground, she could see the face of Sarah Baker looking up, half masked by the loud-hailer, as she bawled up instructions that were drowned out by the screaming of the accident siren.

The lift steadied and then, without warning, dropped three meters like a stone. Caught unawares, the driver was thrown sideways. Sections of metal tipped off and hurtled down, clanging and bouncing as they hit the concrete. The driver pitched as the lift stopped with a jerk and a vicious swash, and his head caught the stanchion in front of him. He slumped down and lay helpless.

As the accident siren died to nothing, the amplified voice of Sarah Baker yelled: "Tell him to hold it there! Ladderlift will be there in a minute!"

A minute, Helen decided, was far too long. She looked up as the rope from the hoist sailed down and grabbed. Shoving a loop of rope over her head, round her back and under her arms, she stepped toward the edge.

"Godsake, Commander!" shouted Cohen. "Don't do it!"

She snapped at him. "Get me lowered down to that lift," she ordered, "and make *clear* signals. Now!"

She swung out over the void. Cohen cooperated, and a hundred and more pairs of eyes watched her as she was lowered. The lift swayed dangerously, holding the still form of its driver.

On the floor above steelmen watched, rigid.

"Crazy," muttered one.

"Did what she had to," another said. There was a note of admiration in his voice.

"She *strong* enough?" asked the first.

"Sure."

When she was within a yard of the lift, the coils spat

again, more sparks, more smoke. "Get my shoulders level with it!" she called.

Cohen signaled for lowering. "Don't get any part of you *under* it!" he screeched.

Then she was level. The unconscious driver was within her grasp. She grabbed him under the armpits and hauled him toward her. The lift kicked again and hit her in the stomach. She gasped and hung on, heaved herself forward, wrenched the unconscious man to her and at last clasped her hands together round his chest. The lift sagged, spewed smoke and dropped another ten centimeters, and a moment after, she was swinging in midair with the driver hanging limply in her grasp.

She began to be hauled up.

Below, Baker turned her attention to the rescue squad, whose articulated vehicle was approaching, its hooter bellowing for clearance.

She waved an arm and shouted, "Get a support under this before it drops!"

She watched the truck skid to a halt ten meters away from her, shedding blue-helmeted men as it slowed. She watched the truck, and in that moment, the antigrav lift fell.

Those in the engine area of V.12 did not see it, as they were concentrating on the pulling to safety of Lieutenant Commander Lindstrom and her burden, but the steelmen saw it, and so did the rescue men on the ground.

The lift fell, but not vertically. It was as though, in its final surrender to the forces against which it spent its life battling, the lift found a small, unbalanced fraction of power before its final burnout. That fraction of power was sufficient to make it sway three meters out of the vertical before it dropped the last ten meters like a stone. It collapsed Baker's lean body as though it were a plasticene doll, and the lift smashed into the concrete with a harsh rasp of rending metal, giving a final shower of sparks which bedizened, in grotesque horrors, the blood which seeped from under it in a sluggish stream, seeking the oblivion of a drainage channel as though it were a living part of some shameful, sensate evil.

Helen was no more than the height of two men from the solid ground now, still clutching her unconscious burden, and she was clearly out of danger. She reached the ground, delivering the lift driver into waiting hands. She struggled to unloop the holding rope. Free at last, she rushed to the fallen lift, where the rescue squad were trying to hook the wreck to a truck crane.

Near her feet, the red spring ran from beneath the wreckage.

Helen turned away, her eyes dimmed with tears—tears unbecoming to an officer of the corps. This was the way the world ended for the woman who had once been the "Star Dancer"; this was the finish of all the hard, bitter years.

THUNDER OF STARS

If it's justice they seek, then justice
they'll get,
All strictly according to law;
It may take a week, but they'll
straighten 'em yet,
As long as it's good for the Corps.

Did he insult the police? Did he
bilk a hotel?
A crewman could do this, and more—
But be out on release, have his fine
paid as well,
As long as it's good for the Corps.

Did you dare to suggest that a
spaceman can fail?
Did you criticize, then, not adore?
Oh, the Med/Psyche will test, and
correctively jail,
For that would be good for the Corps!

(Scurrilous verse published in humorous magazine PRIVATE SCAN May 2162.)

LIEUTENANT SUSAN Pringle was seated at her desk, her attention divided between the morning newscast which was appearing on the wall screen opposite and the documents and folders in front of her which bore the stamp of the Judge Advocate General's Branch.

" . . . Supreme Court Judge Alote Jones, who has

been appointed to take charge of the *Athena* inquiry . . ." the screen voice was saying.

She looked up to see the judge, a large, stern-looking African in middle age, talking to an interviewer. It was clearly an unequal contest. For three whole minutes the judge managed to say almost nothing, and yet at the same time to give an impression of infinite wisdom. The one thing he *did* say was that, in dealing with the *Athena* inquiry, he had absolute right in law to make whatever rulings he chose and to admit any evidence he thought fit.

"But surely, Your Honor, might this not be interpreted as a despotic attitude?" asked the interviewer.

Alote Jones quelled him with a haughty look. "I am not interested in interpretations of my actions. *I* am unimportant. What really matters is that, with God's help and a minimum of bickering, we should arrive at the truth of this incident, and that the blame—if there be any blame—should be placed squarely where it belongs. You have asked your last question."

Pringle decided that she liked Alote Jones. He had a certain style. Was he, she wondered, quite as incorruptible as he appeared to be? She hoped so.

The door opened smartly and Admiral Carter came in. She made to switch off the wall screen, but Carter shook his head.

"Keep it on, Pringle. I missed the earlier news."

"Did you talk to Commander Bruce?" she asked.

Carter nodded, his eyes watching the screen.

"Are you sure that was wise, at this stage?"

He turned to face her, head sunk deep between his heavy shoulders. "I tell you this, Pringle. I've never been neutral in my life and I'm not proposing to start now. Tom Bruce is a stiff-necked bastard, but he's a damned good officer, and he's right. And I'm talking, if they give me a chance to talk, on that basis. Did you see that Excelsior lawyer dripping out his poison in last night's "Solar View?" I'm willing to bet you a month's pay that he has men out right now, bribing and intimidating people to reinforce his dirty slurs."

"I heard what he said about the Corps," Pringle said. "I thought it was quite unnecessarily vicious."

"Unnecessarily?" grunted Carter. "Not with that boy. He knows where he's aiming. The Corps is law, once you leave Earth. Give them a chance and they'll all be snapping round us, trying to destroy the position of trust and authority we've built up. Make no mistake, girl, this Morton has allies, even though they may not have shown themselves yet. Once this thing gets started, you watch out for the corruption and cozenage. I only hope the judge—"

"He was on just now—" Pringle stopped as Carter motioned urgently with his hand, moved forward toward the screen and turned up the sound.

" . . . and the President is now resting peacefully. The operation has gone according to plan, under the direction of Space Corps Surgeon-General, Admiral Karl Hurwitz, assisted by Commander Bolkovsky and Lieutenant Commander Chan. A further bulletin will be issued at 23.59 hours Moon Standard Time."

"So *that's* the story behind the moon inspection trip," Carter said. "No wonder Henry Fong was being cagey." All at once he sagged, seemed older.

"You're worrying again," Pringle said.

"You're damned right I'm worrying," Carter said, straightening his shoulders with an effort. "Bruce talked to the President before he destroyed *Athena*, but there's no record of the conversation. We may need the old man's personal testimony—need it badly if things get too rough."

"I've had the files from the JAG's department," Pringle said.

Carter grunted. "Right. I suppose I'd better take a look. Maybe this Persian bull, Sharva or whatever his name is, will be able to handle that snake Morton. He comes highly recommended." Grabbing the bundle of documents, he barged through into the inner office.

He was seated at his desk, poring through the material, when the vidphone buzzed. He muttered a curse and switched it on.

"Junius," said his wife. "There you are. I've been trying to—"

"Velma," he began. "I'm not—"

"Now you listen to me, Junius," she commanded. "I hope you're not thinking of coming home, are you?"

He hadn't imagined that she could surprise him, ever, but she did. The Admiral gaped like a landed fish. "Wha . . . what?"

"Don't you come home here," ordered Velma Carter. "Don't you think of resting or taking time off now; you can't afford to!"

"I can't?"

"Certainly not! With the *Athena* inquiry coming up you've got important work to do there. Pitch in, Junius, and tell 'em about the Corps, about the job people like Bruce and Lindstrom are doing. Remind these civilians what *semper ducens* means!"

Carter gazed owlishly at his wife's plump, still attractive face, then he began to chuckle. The chuckle became open laughter, and Lieutenant Pringle, who had just entered the room, stood watching in amazement.

"Sure, Velma," he said. "I'll stay, don't worry. And Velma . . ."

"Yes?" she said warily.

"I love you," he said. "You're the best wife I ever had." He switched off and looked up at Pringle. "Yes?"

"Admiral Mariano's here," she said. "He says he has to see you right away."

"Hell!" snarled Carter, his good humor gone like a puff of smoke in a breeze. "All right, send him in."

Mariano marched into the office and halted sharply in front of Carter's desk. He looked annoyed.

"Longcloud, Commander Charles Longcloud," he said, without preliminary.

"Yes?" frowned Carter, momentarily puzzled.

"According to Corps General Orders of this date, Commander Charles Longcloud, 2 i/c Space College has been temporarily seconded to Moon Commander in order to carry out investigation on meteor incidence in the perimeter station areas."

Carter said: "The order certainly didn't come from me, as you can very easily verify through your well-known network of pen-pushing spy-eyes."

"No. It came, in fact, from the President's office," Mariano said.

"Then maybe you should take it up with *him*?" Carter was enjoying himself.

"But Longcloud was scheduled to be interviewed by the Commissioning Board, with a view to his appointment as Commander of *Venturer Twelve*," said Mariano. "The President's office should have been informed of this fact."

"Fact?" Carter rumbled, his face darkening.

Mariano said: "We've got to have a commander for *Venturer Twelve*, and now the other man is out of the running."

Carter reared to his feet, dark and terrible. "What in hell's name do you mean, out of the running?" he roared.

Mariano was not without courage, but he moved back a pace. "Junius, let's be realistic about this thing," he said placatingly. "I know how you feel about Bruce, but he's been unfortunate. The press is already calling him a mass murderer, by implication. Right or wrong, the public isn't going to forget such charges in a hurry, even if he comes out of the inquiry without an official blemish on his character."

"Damn the public," barked Carter.

"In the last resort you, I, the President, Bruce—we're all *their* servants." Mariano sounded quite sincere.

Carter's eyes narrowed as he glared at the trim uniformed figure in front of him. "Humility sits badly on all that gold braid, Mariano," he said quietly.

"Most of the population must already have made up their minds about Bruce."

"And what you're suggesting is that we should endorse their stupid, ignorant judgment of a good man by dropping him from consideration as commander of *Venturer Twelve*?"

"Junius, this has been a purely internal Corps matter so far. Nobody outside the Commission even knows that Bruce is being considered for the post."

"In that case . . ." Carter pressed a button on his desk. Pringle appeared.

"Pringle—got your notebook? Good girl!" he said, baring his uneven teeth in an unholy grin. "I want to dictate a press release."

"Junius!" Mariano's smoothness was completely gone now.

"Good day, *Rear* Admiral," Carter said. "You will be informed when your presence is required for a meeting of the Commissioning Board. Until then, I'd be obliged if you would go back to whatever work you have on hand, and let me get on with mine. Now, Pringle—a press release. 'To representatives of all media, from the office of the Chairman of the Commissioning Board, *Venturer Twelve.* It was announced today that a decision will very soon be made in the matter of filling the one remaining vacancy in the establishment of *Venturer Twelve*; that of Commander. It was disclosed that the man most likely to fill that post is Lieutenant Commander Thomas Winford Bruce, at present CC System Patrols . . .' "

There was a moment of silence, then Pringle, her stylus poised over her notebook, said: "Is that all, sir?"

Carter grinned, hunching his shoulders. "I think that will be enough, don't you Mariano?"

Rear Admiral Sylvano Mariano, his fine Latin nostrils twitching, glared down for a moment at the self-congratulatory, gnomelike figure, then with a smart about turn, he marched out of the office.

Carter chuckled.

"Could I have your attention please, Commander Lindstrom?" said Senior Lieutenant Sharva of the Judge Advocate General's department. "If there are any points of discrepancy, now is the time for us to iron them out."

Helen turned from the window, where she had been gazing out unseeingly at the expanse of the System Patrol spaceport, and faced the big, dark lawyer. "I'm listening," she said, aware that the green eyes of Tom Bruce, who was seated behind his desk, were regarding her watchfully.

"This inquiry is going to be loaded with emotion," said Lieutenant Sharva. "One word, one gesture out of place and the whole thing could blow up in our faces. That is why it is essential that you should both be completely frank with me now."

"You have our statements." Bruce ignited a cigar impatiently. "Do you consider them unsatisfactory?"

"No, not as far as they go," Sharva said.

"There is some dispute about the facts, then?" Bruce said.

Sharva examined his big hands. He was careful,

precise without being pedantic. "What I'm talking about are human attitudes, emotional interpretations of the facts."

Tom Bruce mashed the cigar in the ashtray; he was irritated. "Lieutenant Sharva, I'm an officer of Space Corps. If you want emotional interpretation you'd better get yourself an actor."

Sharva's dark eyes appealed to Helen, and she, despite her determination, found herself involved.

"Tom, you've got to appreciate what the Lieutenant is implying," she said. "Whether you'll admit it or not, when that inquiry starts, in the eyes of the world *we're* going to be on trial. We killed five hundred people."

"Lieutenant, I make no apologies for what I did, and I intend to make no apologies in court," Bruce said harshly. "I killed five hundred people, yes. But by doing so I saved the lives of perhaps fifteen million."

He reared up from behind his desk, thrusting his chair away so that it crashed to the floor. "*Christ*, woman!" he snapped at Helen. "You, of all people, should know, should understand! That decision, once made, had to be beyond question!"

"Even in your own mind?" she said.

"Especially there, if I'm going to go on living and remain sane."

She looked into his face. She knew now the tensions that had etched those deep lines on either side of his jaw, the resolution that made the strong chin jut at that precise angle, the determination that held the hardness in those clear, green eyes. And she was ashamed, ashamed to have imagined that she, or Sarah Baker, had a monopoly of loneliness and suffering.

Sharva met her eyes steadily. "Commander Lindstrom," he said, sternly. "It is essential that we three, at least, are clear on one point. Whatever impression the Corporation lawyers, or the representatives of the colonists, may attempt to give, this is to be an inquiry, not a trial. If you're in any doubt, remember the fact that, had it not been for an act of piracy on the part of the colonists aboard *Athena*, that ship would have been in hyperspace now, a quarter of the way to Hegenis Three. Now: shall we proceed?"

Carter had called him "the Persian bull." Helen felt a new respect growing in her for this great dark man. He might not have deep space experience, but he understood his own work thoroughly. Tom Bruce seemed to feel the same way. There were no further arguments as they went carefully through the testimony.

Hurwitz came in, pink, unruffled, serious of face. With him was World Admiral Hoffner, stepping like an elephant unwilling to break eggs.

"Just for a minute, Joe. No more," said Hurwitz.

Hoffner came to the bed and looked down at the small, aged face of Oharo. "Well," he whispered grudgingly, "he's breathing, anyway."

"You say the damndest things!" Hurwitz was annoyed.

Hoffner grunted. "One thing that keeps nagging at me is that inquiry starting the day after tomorrow, or is it tomorrow?"

Hurwitz said seriously, "If you're expecting some intervention from him, forget it."

"Not intervention . . ."

"*What* then?"

"Bruce talked to the President before he blasted that ship."

"We both know that." Hurwitz showed signs of impatience.

"Yes, but how do we get corroboration of what the President said?"

Hurwitz was slightly bewildered. "Why do you need

corroboration of anything? The inquiry will have the word of a senior officer about what took place—isn't that enough?"

"Not for what's going to happen down there," Hoffner said. "They'll question whether he really spoke to the President, and even if the President gave his authority for what happened, they still won't be satisfied, some of 'em." He spoke urgently. "Come out of your white, aseptic nest, Karl, and understand what really goes on. That won't be just Tom Bruce down there on the stand, it will be the whole Corps. I think maybe I'd better have a talk with Henry Fong."

THUNDER OF STARS

As far as I am aware, there is not the slightest justification for secret hearings of any kind in the normal civilian practices of justice, and I would be very wary of any special pleading on behalf of police or space corps. There can be few cases where any submission for special consideration in such matters does not indicate a weakness which would be best exposed to public scrutiny!

(His Honor Alote Jones.
Extract from speech on
his appointment as World
Supreme Court Judge.)

THE PRESIDENT of the Excelsior Corporation bent his bald head over the document. "Where did you get hold of this?" he demanded, looking up half a minute later.

"Through a certain contact in Space Corps Records," Morton said. "It seems to me to have direct bearing on *any* decision made by Lieutenant Commander Bruce—don't you agree?"

"You'll be crucifying the man," Elkan Niebohr said quietly.

"Possibly," Alger Morton said confidently. "But I shall make my point." It amused him to see the obvious distaste on the old man's face, because he knew that however much Niebohr tried to maintain the benevolent 'Uncle Elkan' image, deep down he was still tied to the ruthless code that had allowed him to fight his way to the top, and the knowledge that even now he was not high enough to afford the luxury of a conscience.

Helen Lindstrom arrived at the stage door of the Edward Kennedy Ellington Concert Hall shortly after ten. The security man who examined her pass handed her over to a dumpy, mouse-haired PO with JAG department flashes on the sleeves of her uniform.

"Good morning, Commander Lindstrom." The PO saluted stiffly. "If you'll follow me, please. Lieutenant Sharva is in Monitor Room Fifteen."

"Thank you." Helen acknowledged the salute and fell into step beside the PO. The traffic in the thickly carpeted corridors was heavy; it consisted largely of serious-faced, soberly dressed civilians carrying briefcases.

She wondered if Tom Bruce had arrived yet. She had looked out for him in the dining room at the hotel, both at dinner the previous night and at breakfast that morning, half hoping that they would meet by chance, but she had not caught sight of him. She had wondered several times whether or not to call his room. But she hadn't called him, partly because she wasn't certain that talk would suffice; and partly, she admitted to herself grudgingly, out of stubborn pride. If he wanted her, then *he* would have to be the one who called.

"Here we are, Commander," the PO said. She rapped on a cream-colored door, then opened it and stood respectfully to one side. The major part of one wall of the room was taken up by three large TV screens each of which showed a different view of the big auditorium. Beneath this was a videotape console. The other furnishings of the room consisted of half a dozen chairs, a couple of free-standing ashtrays and a water cooler.

"She recognized the expression on Tom Bruce's face the moment she entered the room. The green eyes narrowed, the chin jutting out at an arrogant angle, and the muscular body tensed forward; the combination was as clear as a gale warning. He and Sharva stood facing each other like two well-matched gladiators.

"Good morning, Commander Lindstrom," Sharva said, half turning toward her and smiling briefly.

Bruce acknowledged her presence with a curt nod and plunged back into the argument that her appearance had interrupted. He waved one hand in the direction of the TV screen.

"I don't give a damn what you say, Sharva! My place, and that of Commander Lindstrom, is down there, in the body of the court, where we can hear what is being said and see everything that goes on."

Sharva's voice was low pitched, carefully modulated, patient. "At the present stage of the proceedings, the presence of either or both of you in the courtroom can be of little assistance. As you know, the press and the TV networks have not been idle; and a large number of the people down there in the courtroom will have already prejudged the issue."

"Then what possible chance have we of a fair hearing?" Helen said.

"A good question." Sharva grinned, showing an oversized but perfect set of white teeth. "Let me put it to you this way: His Honor, Judge Alote Jones, will make use of the first day, at least, to put on such a calculated display of the majesty and pomp of the law as to make even the hotheads pause and reconsider their position. Keeping the proceedings as nearly as possible on an impersonal level, he will make it his business systematically to scare the hell out of anyone who comes here with the intention of making a three-ring circus out of *his* inquiry. I know the way Alote Jones works."

"That sounds reasonable, Tom," Helen said.

"That's only one way of looking at it," Bruce said, scowling. "The other interpretation—and one which won't be slow in finding followers—is that we're afraid to show our faces."

"There will be plenty of opportunity for that later," Sharva said. "Judge Jones agreed that, in the first instance, the interests of the inquiry will best be served by using the recording rather than personal testimony. Bear this in mind; if you were to give your testimony in person at this stage, Morton would be perfectly within his rights to request an immediate cross-examination."

Tom Bruce's face darkened. "So—what the hell? I've got nothing to hide. I'd welcome the chance of meeting that snake face to face after the way he's been shooting his mouth off on TV and in the press."

"That," said Sharva, calmly, "is *precisely* my point. Morton is an expert in the business of goading witnesses. Five minutes on the stand with you and he'd have you blowing your top, with the whole world looking on. On the other hand, if your testimony is confined to the recording, he can do nothing more than comment briefly on your report."

"But if we're right . . ." Tom Bruce began.

"The longer I can delay calling you to the stand, the longer I shall have to observe Morton in action and to analyze his method of attack. Make no mistake about it, *attack he will*."

"You make it sound like a game of chess, Sharva."

"It is a deadly game." The big Persian glanced at the wall-screen. "And now if you'll excuse me? I'll join you again during the first recess."

For all his bulk, the dark man moved gracefully. Helen watched appreciatively as he walked out of the room.

"Damned . . . lawyer," growled Tom Bruce.

"Damned good lawyer, is my guess," Helen said. "I think we'll do well to take notice of what he says."

"You may be right, but I never was one for sitting back in an observation post when there's some action in progress."

"You'll get your action before this thing's over," Helen said. She turned her attention to the TV. The screens in Monitor Room Fifteen showed the pictures being put out by the three main TV networks, each available with its own commentary.

Helen turned up the volume and found herself a chair, one removed from Bruce's.

" ... choice of this great concert hall was something of a surprise," said the commentator as the camera panned the interior of the building. "It had originally been expected that the inquiry would be held in the Palace of Justice main courtroom. However, it is Judge Alote Jones' stated policy in this matter that the close relatives of the deceased colonists have an inalienable right to attend the inquiry in person, and there would certainly not have been room for such a large body of people at the Palace of Justice. Here, on the other hand, it has been possible to reserve the entire first balcony for them ..."

"From which they will no doubt spend most of their time howling for our blood," Tom Bruce said.

"Not with Alote Jones presiding," Helen replied. "Everybody will get a hearing, but he won't stand for any nonsense."

The voice of the commentator continued: "As you will see, half the body of the hall has been cleared of seats to make room for the various legal representatives, their staff and equipment. The judiciary will be seated on the apron stage, which is fitted over the broad orchestral pit. The evidence programmer is installed in a special booth to their right, from which he will control the pictures to be projected on the giant screen at the back of the stage.

"The legal representatives are now in their places, and I understand that the doors have just been opened at the first balcony entrance . . ."

The picture zoomed in on the first balcony. Eighteen stern-faced men came in and took up separate places, distributing themselves in accordance with some prearranged plan.

"See what I mean?" Helen said. "Alote Jones isn't taking any chances."

More people were flooding onto the balcony now. There were faces from Greenland, from Indonesia, from Africa, from India, from every part of Earth. Many were shabbily dressed and ill nourished. Helen reflected that, despite his achievements, there was still some conquering for Man to do, right here on his home planet.

The camera picked out individual faces. Most of them had one thing in common—an aggrieved grayness, a sullen quality which showed that they had been hit, hurt and bitterly deprived. They had come to see justice done before they flooded in their claims for compensation.

The commentator continued: "Now the court is assembled, except for the presiding judge and his assistants . . ."

An usher called for silence. "His Honor, World Supreme Court Judge Alote Jones." The court rose, all faces turned toward the stage.

Judge Alote Jones, a big man, impressive in his purple robes, appeared from the wings and walked to the center. He paused for a moment, looking up toward the first balcony, then took his seat. There was a rustling and a slight murmur as the court followed suit.

The camera was close in on the solemn dark face of

Alote Jones as he outlined his aims in an unhesitating deep voice. "Our purpose here is to arrive at the true facts in what has become known as the *Athena Affair*. And this, I repeat, is our only purpose.

"If there is any attempt made to hide that truth, be assured that I shall take strong measures against whomsoever may be responsible. Moreover, I charge all news services not to color, emphasize, or reslant any evidence that may be given here. The whole proceedings of the inquiry will be broadcast live, and selection of any kind is forbidden. Commentators may summarize for the benefit of their viewers, but they will *not* interpret or opinionate. To this end, I would publicly remind all media that all information transmitted on this inquiry is being monitored by officials of World Judiciary."

Alote Jones paused and looked round the packed hall. His audience was silent; the only sound was the whirring of electronic gear. "Are there any questions?"

In the near silence, one sound contributed materially to the rising tension, the sound of a woman sobbing.

"Very well," the judge said, at length. "It is now my duty to appoint the members of the bench who will assist me in this inquiry." He consulted a list. "I have nominated the following: Spyros Venizelos, President of North American Electronics."

A tall, graying man came forward, bowed to the judge, and sat down.

"Sergei Rubashov, Chief Circuit Judge, Eastern Asia." A thickset, bald man, wearing robes similar to those of Judge Jones, bowed and took his place.

"Eric Akersson, Chairman of the World Union of Space Technicians." A lean, blond man in his late thirties appeared, nodded to the judge and sat down.

"And Elena Marx, Professor of Physics at the University of Paris." Professor Marx was small, gray and tiny. She walked slowly with the help of two arthritic's tripod sticks.

"Representing the Space Corps, I have selected two able officers of high reputation, Admiral Samuel Lincoln Suvorov and Rear-Admiral Sylvano Mariano."

"Mariano!" Tom Bruce, watching the monitor screen, snorted his disgust. "Only two Space Corps members on the judiciary, and Jones has to pick that damned finagler!"

"Finagler, perhaps, but in a situation like this, he's all Corps," Helen said.

"I wish I had your faith," Bruce said dourly. He ground out his cigar.

THUNDER OF STARS

. . . Do not count stars;
They are as grains of sand.
Do not be deluded
That here is love, and faith,
And everlasting truth;
Do not be suborned, and think you hear
The message of eternity.
Hell is black, infinite, sparkling.
Hell is worth avoiding.

(THE LIARS : I. Kavanin.)

LIEUTENANT SHARVA was the first of the legal representatives to make a preliminary statement. He stood, tall and dark, massive as an oak, speaking with quiet confidence. What he said was a model of conciseness.

"Your Honor, the position of the Space Corps in this matter is clearly based on one premise. Had the *Athena* been allowed to continue on the course she was following after the blowup of her engines, then she would inevitably have plunged to Earth. She had become, in effect, a deadly missile of enormous mass and devastating speed, pointed at one of the most densely populated areas of our planet. We have reliable estimates that as a result of such an impact at least fifteen million lives would have been lost. There was therefore no alternative but to destroy *Athena*.

"In support of this, we shall present reports from Corps and civilian tracking stations on Moon, Mars and Earth; recordings of conversations between Commander Bruce's ship and these stations, made at the time of the emergency; and Commander Bruce's own official report, transmitted to Corps HQ immediately after the destruction of *Athena*. As Your Honor has already pointed out, there has been a great deal of careless talk and deliberately angled comment on the subject of this affair. Commander Bruce did not lightly take his decision to destroy *Athena*. He acted in good faith, on the basis of the facts presented to him. He acted in the sincere belief that, however terrible the results of his action, they would be infinitely less terrible than the alternative."

"Good for you, Lieutenant!" said Helen Lindstrom as Sharva resumed his seat.

"Don't start cheering yet," Tom Bruce said. "It's going to be a long war."

"Thank you, Lieutenant Sharva," said Judge Alote Jones. He rapped his gavel on the bench in front of him to quell a growing murmur of conversation. "Mr. Morton?"

"Your Honor." Morton rose to his feet and bowed. Slim, sharp featured, he stood for a long moment looking round the court, his gaze lingering for a moment on the crowded balcony, before turning to face the judiciary. "Your Honor, I would like to congratulate Lieutenant Sharva on the brevity and clarity of his opening address and thank him for his statement of the basic premise on which rests the position of the Space Corps. However, I feel obliged to point out that he has in truth presented us *not* with a basic premise, but an *assumption*—this arrogant assumption that an organization composed of ordinary human beings is incapable of doing wrong, or committing any error; and further, even more dangerous, the extension of this assumption to cover the actions of any single member of the Corps to the point of demanding immunity for him.

"I have no doubt that Lieutenant Sharva will produce, as promised, all the data necessary to prove beyond a shadow of doubt that if unchecked, *Athena* would have crashed into Earth, causing the havoc he has suggested. But I would ask you all to bear in mind most earnestly that these will be Space Corps figures, produced by Space Corps experts in support of a Space Corps decision."

It was at this point that Judge Alote Jones broke in. "Mr. Morton, you will confine your remarks to a statement of the position of the Excelsior Corporation. If you have nothing to say in this respect, please have the goodness to sit down."

"That's telling *him*," Helen said approvingly.

Bruce grunted. "Too damned late. He's already drawn blood."

Down in the court, Alger Morton inclined his head in the direction of the judiciary. "My apologies, Your Honor. I had no intention of wasting the court's time; I wished merely to draw its attention to the existence of this particularly large sacred cow."

Alote Jones rapped his gavel, his black face heavy with anger. "Mr. Morton! I'll have no more of this line."

"As Your Honor pleases," Morton said with a deliberately mocking formality. "Now, with regard to the position of my corporation in this matter. In order that this should be fully apparent, I am forced to move back to the time before *Athena* left Earth, when the passengers who were on that last, ill-fated voyage were in the process of selection.

"At this time, the man Persoons—who was the self-confessed ringleader in the act of piracy which resulted in the takeover of *Athena* by the colonists—made what have since been proved to be a number of completely false statements during interviews with Excelsior Corporation officials. Not only did he make false statements about his past record, but he also produced forged references as to his past employment, character and background . . ."

Judge Jones intervened, yet again. "In that case, Mr. Morton, surely he should never have been allowed to board the ship in the first place?"

"Your Honor, there is little doubt of the truth of that statement," Morton said. "Unfortunately, my corporation was not aware at the time of the false statements and references."

Judge Jones said: "Mr. Morton, under the terms of its charter granted by the Colonization Supervision Committee, your corporation is bound to take all possible measures to verify any statements made by a potential colonist, *before* allowing him to sign a contract."

"That is perfectly true, Your Honor," Morton said.

"And yet you still admit that the man, Persoons' references were not checked?" Alote Jones said. "Surely you must offer some explanation for this omission?"

"I can offer explanation," Morton said smoothly. "In theory, Your Honor is quite correct, all references and all statements made by potential colonists *should* be checked.

"However, the Excelsior Corporation deals with up to ten thousand individual colonists during a year. To check out each one of these people completely would necessitate the employment of a massive force of inquiry agents and enormous expenditure. Our security branch has therefore evolved a system by which a random sample of files is checked out completely."

"How large is that sample, Mr. Morton?" demanded Alote Jones.

"Unfortunately, I do not have those figures at hand," Morton said blandly.

There was a sudden buzz of discussion in the court.

Alote Jones rapped his gavel and said: "It is my impression that by such a breach of the conditions of its charter, the Excelsior Corporation renders itself liable to the payment of a considerable penalty."

"With respect, Your Honor, the Excelsior Corporation is fully aware of that fact, and I make this admission with the full knowledge and backing of my board of directors," Morton said. "Many a man who has achieved nothing but failure here on Earth has gone out to the colonization planets and become a successful and respected member of that colony. If the Excelsior Corporation is in error in this matter, it is surely an error on the side of humanity?"

"The clever bastard!" said Tom Bruce, pushing his chair back noisily and rising to his feet in disgust. "If Sharva's going to beat *him*, he'll need to use a club!"

Morton had resumed his seat, an expression of satisfaction on his thin face, and Judge Alote Jones was announcing a recess. Helen turned the sound down and turned to face Bruce.

"He'll pull something out of the bag when the time comes," she said.

"He'd *better*!" Bruce growled, pacing the small room, hands slapping the side seams of his trousers as he strove to release some of the pent-up anger that seethed in his body. "I underestimated Morton. Take that admission about their failure to check Persoons' references, for instance; even if the CSC slap a fine of half a million credits on Excelsior, Morton knows damned well that he'll be getting value for money. Excelsior Corporation, the people's friend, the big-hearted corporation that gives the little men a break. And opposing that, the Space Corps, an impersonal, military organization that destroys five hundred people at one swipe and makes no apology."

"Tom, it's only a beginning," Helen protested.

"And a bloody bad one at that!" Bruce said. "Sharva's out of his class."

"Thank you for the vote of confidence, Commander Bruce," said Lieutenant Sharva. He had entered the room during Bruce's last speech. Now he stood, massive and dignified, his dark eyes regarding Bruce steadily.

"Commander Bruce didn't mean . . ." Helen, flushed with embarrassment, moved to avert the impending clash.

"Dont make apologies for me, Helen," Tom Bruce said, his jaw jutting forward as he glared at Sharva. "Morton made rings round him down there, and Sharva knows it."

Sharva replied, still miraculously calm. "Morton has started by pulling out all the emotional stops he can think of. Surely when we come down to dealing in plain facts, he's going to find something of an anticlimax on his hands?"

"Unless he's holding something in reserve that we don't know about yet," Bruce said. He flung out his right arm in an impatient gesture. "Ah, what the hell's the use of chewing it over? I'm going to have a drink, and maybe some lunch. Coming, Helen?"

"That's one of the things I came to tell you," Sharva said. "We have an invitation to lunch. The Presidential secretary called me straight after the session ended. There's a flycar waiting for us right now."

"Henry Fong?" Bruce said. "I wonder what the old fox wants."

Sharva shrugged his heavy shoulders. "I don't know, but that invitation sounded mighty like an order to me. Shall we go?"

Helen settled in the well-sprung chair and reflected that in this amiable, post-lunch mood Henry Fong looked more than ever like a slimmed-down Buddha in modern dress. The meal had been delicate and civilized, Chinese cooking at its best, served by Fong's manservant, in his own unostentatiously luxurious penthouse apartment. Conversation during the meal had ranged over a wide area of interests; in particular Helen had been impressed by the evident erudition of Lieutenant Sharva on the subject of Oriental philosophy, in the discussion of which he had more than held his own with Henry Fong, one of the world's foremost authorities. Tom Bruce had been silent.

The Presidential secretary made a steeple of his slender, beautifully manicured hands and beamed at each of his guests in turn. "Brandy, Commander Lindstrom? Or would you prefer something sweeter—a Cointreau, perhaps?" Helen declined, smiling, and he turned his attention to Bruce. "Commander? Brandy? Good." He motioned to his manservant. "And for Lieutenant Sharva, perhaps another cup of coffee?"

"Thank you, sir," Sharva said.

Fong waited patiently until his guests had been served and the manservant had left the room before speaking again. Although there had been no previous mention of the inquiry whatsoever, he made no preliminaries. "Now, Sharva; as I understand it, Judge Jones has decided against a preliminary address on the part of Mr. Zakoyan. Is that correct?"

Sharva lowered his coffee cup. "Yes, sir. It was his ruling that, at this stage, Zakoyan must hold merely a watching brief for the colonists' relatives. He may be given an opportunity to address the court at a later stage, when the facts are established to the satisfaction of the judiciary."

Fong examined the fingernails of his right hand with approval. "Yes . . . a sound man, Alote Jones, if a mite stolid. But then stolidity may very well be a prime virtue in a Supreme Court Judge, don't you think?" The question hung in the air for a moment, but his listeners gauged correctly that it was purely rhetorical and maintained a respectful silence. "I take it then that the main purpose of this afternoon's session will be the presentation of the Corps testimony?"

"Yes, sir, commencing with the playing of Commander Bruce's report," Sharva said.

"Yes," breathed Fong, maintaining the sibilant as he gazed blandly at his listeners. "A commendably terse and well-considered tape. However . . ."

"I gave the facts as I saw them," Bruce said, leaning slightly forward in his chair as he eyed Fong keenly.

Fong nodded benevolently. "You did indeed, Commander. However, I have taken the liberty of supplying the evidence programmer at the inquiry with a lightly edited version of the original."

His listeners could hardly have been more startled if he had grown a second head. The three of them gazed at him for a moment in complete astonishment.

Sharva was the first to speak: "Do I understand you correctly, sir? You have tampered with official Space Corps evidence?"

Henry Fong smiled as he raised his hands for silence. He turned his attention to Bruce. "Commander, when the fate of the *Athena* was still in some doubt, you contacted Moon Base and spoke to the President."

"That is so," Bruce said, frowning.

"And you explained the situation?"

"As well as I could, under the circumstances; there was very little time to be wasted," Bruce said. "I told the President that if it turned out that the *Athena* was on collision course with Earth, as we suspected, then the only course of action if we were to avoid the greatest disaster in the history of the human race would be to destroy *Athena* and the people aboard her."

"And the President's reply to this suggestion?"

"He merely confirmed that, as Corps officer on the spot, I must follow the dictates of my own conscience and come to my own decision on the basis of the facts presented to me."

"And you were satisfied by this advice?"

"This was an emergency, Mr. Fong," Bruce said, his voice developing a sudden edge. "A decision had to be made."

"And you were the one who had to make it?"

"Yes."

"In that case," Henry Fong said, "I must confess myself slightly mystified. Why did you find it necessary to call the President to obtain confirmation of something you knew in the first place—that the decision rested with you?"

"I simply felt that it was the right thing to do," Bruce said.

"Or did you, perhaps, feel that by obtaining such an endorsement from the President you were insuring yourself against the consequences of a possible wrong decision?" said Fong.

Tom Bruce was bolt upright in his chair now, his green eyes wide with anger as he stared at the imperturbable Henry Fong. "Mr. Secretary, you have no right to make such an assumption! I must ask you—"

Fong raised one slim hand. "All right, Commander, please don't take the suggestion seriously. I merely put it to you at this point as an illustration."

"An illustration of *what*?"

"Of the kind of questions that would undoubtedly have been put to you in the course of the inquiry by Morton, and/or possibly Zakoyan, had the original version of your report, with its reference to your conversation with the President, been allowed to stand,"

Fong said. "This reference is not included in the otherwise identical tape, which is now in the hands of the evidence programmer; and not you, Commander Lindstrom or Lieutenant Sharva will make any statement in public or private that might in any way involve the President's name in this affair. Should he fail to survive the present crisis, no possible advantage can be gained for anyone by smearing his memory by association with the *Athena* affair; and should he, God willing, survive, it will be equally essential that his present saintly image should be maintained. If it were ever to be suggested that this father of the entire human race could be associated with a decision to kill five hundred of his children, the consequences would be disastrous."

"You realize that you may be asking Commander Bruce to sacrifice his reputation, career, perhaps even his life, by demanding this?" Sharva said. "Morton has already made considerable attacks and is no doubt preparing others. Without the President's backing he stands alone and undefended."

"You underestimate yourself, Lieutenant," Fong said blandly.

"I'm sorry, Mr. Secretary, but I cannot take your view," Sharva persisted. "Commander Bruce has the right to—"

"All right, Sharva," Tom Bruce said suddenly. "As far as I'm concerned there's no question about what has to be done. I'm prepared to accept Mr. Fong's request that the President should not be brought into this matter. I'm content to let the facts speak for themselves, without any special pleading."

Henry Fong rose to his feet. "Commander Bruce, I expected nothing less of you; but, on behalf of the President and all those who depend on him, thank you."

The afternoon session of the inquiry began with the playing of Tom Bruce's report tape. This was followed by reports from the tracking-station operators involved in the operation. The technical reports did not make for drama and the entire hall seemed to be sinking into an uninterested lethargy. What, in the morning, had promised to be a large-scale clash of opposing forces was now settling into the dull grinding routine of a normal courtroom.

A certain expectancy was regenerated by the appearance of Rear Admiral Junius Farragut Carter on the stand, called there by the judiciary as an expert witness to clarify any points of interpretation arising from the recorded reports. Squat built, red brown of feature and wearing his heavily beribboned dress uniform, Admiral Carter's reputation had preceded him. Here at last, it seemed, was a man who held some potential as a dramatic element. But he disappointed the TV men by answering promptly all questions put to him by the judiciary, unbendingly, acting every inch the part of the correct, sober officer. At length, after conferring among themselves, the judiciary were apparently satisfied, and Judge Jones addressed the legal representative of the Excelsior Corporation. "Do you have any questions to ask of this witness, Mr. Morton?"

"I have indeed, Your Honor."

The Admiral watched Morton's approach with a baleful eye, his weather-beaten face darkening, massive shoulders hunching slightly. A sudden wave of tension swept through the courtroom.

Morton's line of questioning began with a mildness which only served to heighten the anticipation of his listeners.

"Admiral Carter, you appear here in the role of an expert witness on technical matters; however, might I venture to suggest that your long and distinguished career qualified you equally as an authority on matters of Space Corps procedure and disciplinary practice?"

Carter acknowledged the question with a noncommittal grunt.

"In the Space Corps, in contract with other, similar organizations, there would appear to be times when rank is considered of little importance; is this a fact?"

Carter's round, stubbly head seemed to sink farther in between his heavy shoulders as he watched Morton. "Others may advise, may suggest, but each member of the Corps is a highly trained individual, prepared to take complete responsibility in any situation."

"*Any* situation?"

"Mr. Morton, in deep space, or on alien planets, there is no room for formality," Carter said harshly. "Men die out there; suddenly and horribly, they die. Therefore, although the Space Corps must maintain a formal chain of command, it must at the same time make sure that each man or woman of each crew is capable of operating as an efficient individual survival unit."

Morton said: "There seems to me to be some element of paradox involved here. The concept of each member as an individual, decision-making unit appears to be in direct opposition to the idea of 'chain of command.' "

"You, Mr. Morton, are not Space Corps," Carter said, curtly putting the lawyer in his place.

Morton bowed his head briefly with undeceptive humility. "I must ask you to bear with the ignorance of a mere layman and answer my question about this seeming paradox and how it is overcome."

Helen Lindstrom, watching the proceedings on the monitor screen, stirred uneasily. "What's he getting at?" she asked.

Tom Bruce relaxed, lighting another cigar, and said: "Don't worry, old Junius can take care of himself."

Carter eyed his questioner warily. "As in all things, Mr. Morton, there are times when it is necessary to compromise."

"*Compromise*." Morton leapt on the word like a terrier grabbing at a long-awaited rat. "I see, Admiral. Then this system is not, in fact, infallible?"

"I don't follow you."

"Well then, let me put it this way," Morton said. "There must be occasions when, despite training and experience, an individual member of the Corps makes a wrong, even disastrous decision."

The Admiral remained silent, a suspicious gleam in his eye, as he regarded the lawyer. Those who knew Carter recognized the signs of an impending explosion.

Judge Alote Jones intervened. "Please do not waste the court's time on generalities."

"My apologies, Your Honor," Morton said, unruffled. "But if the court will bear with me for a few more minutes, my point will be clear."

The Judge nodded.

Morton turned back to Carter. "Assuming that we are agreed on the point that the Space Corps is made up of human beings, is it not possible that at some time or other, one of these human beings might make a mistaken decision, a wrong judgment?"

"There may be such occasions," Carter said.

"Oh, come now, Admiral, *may* be," pursued Morton. "Surely there must have been at least one such incident during your long career as an officer of Space Corps?"

"Any moment now, Junius is going to blow his top," said Tom Bruce with some relish.

Helen Lindstrom dug her nails into the upholstery of her chair.

Admiral Carter, glaring, cleared his throat loudly. But before he had time to say anything, Morton was in on him again, thrusting home the dart.

"I suggest to you, Admiral, that, in the face of outside investigation, the Corps would maintain its solidarity to the extent of suppressing, even falsifying, any evidence that might be considered damaging to the Corps."

Any answer that Carter might have made was lost, completely drowned in the general uproar that followed the Excelsior lawyer's speech.

"Clever bastard!" growled Tom Bruce as Helen turned down the roaring volume of sound that poured out of the screen. "Alote Jones can rule him out of order, strike what he has said from the record, but as far as the world is concerned he's made his point. By implication, at least, he's discredited any evidence offered by the Space Corps in this inquiry."

"You must be wrong," Helen said. "You've *got* to be. After all, we've two of our own people on the judiciary, Suvorov and Mariano."

"Two out of *seven*," Bruce said.

"Alote Jones . . ."

"Is an ambitious man, bucking for Chief Supreme Court Justice, a post that holds Vice-Presidential status," Bruce said coldly. "He might play the big, bold champion of impartial justice, but in the long run he'll have to bow to popular opinion."

"You're a cynical sod, Tom Bruce," she said.

"No," he said, with a sudden grin. "Just a realist. They're going to nail somebody's hide to the wall—make no mistake about that—and I'm the prime candidate."

"No, Tom, no!" she revolted against his apparent acceptance of defeat. "We were out there in that scout ship together; the responsibility is as much mine as yours."

He leaned forward, grabbing her by the shoulders and digging his strong fingers in until they hurt. "That's not the way we play it in the Corps, Commander," he said. "If you make the slightest attempt to assume any responsibility when you're on the witness stand, I shall scotch you publicly. You were Second in Command of that scout; *I* was the one who made the decisions, and I want no bloody sacrifices from you. Understood?"

His angry, green eyes looked hard into hers for a long moment, then he released his grip. Thrusting her away from him, he strode out of the room.

She watched him go. How could you ever love a man like that? How could you ever get *close* enough?

In space depots, training centers and schools, in installations near enough to get pictures, men and women on and off duty asked: "How much more is he going to dig up?" "What *was* it Bruce did?" "The Kilroy story? That's a fable." "Something in it. Look, Bruce got Star of Honor at Sandpoint, and see how slow his promotion is."

Carter said to Pringle's picture, "So what's in that's new? You been watching the inquiry, girl?"

On the screen, she looked as fresh as she had first thing in the morning. "Me? I have no time for looking at video, sir."

"Like hell," said Carter, pleasantly. "How did we do?"

"I was very impressed by your personality," she answered.

"Leave that," Carter ordered, "and fill me in."

"Verdict on Baker confirmed," she said, becoming more serious. "Death by misadventure. Direction that the whole question of a/g lift maintenance should be gone into."

"Expected," Carter growled. "Next?"

"Space College point out that they are entitled to

send two fourth-year cadets on first trip of *V.12*, and propose to submit names for interview."

"We must bear it. Next?"

"Surgeon-Lieutenant Maseba is still not satisfied with the noise insulation in his sick bays. He has put in a four oh two stroke M."

"*Has* he? He means it, then. Has Chalovsky said anything?"

"Nothing I'd like to repeat, even to you. But Maseba said that he was entitled to make the complaint formal, so he did. He told me that there was nothing personal in it."

"Huh," Carter grunted. "All right, medicos are in a class of their own. We can't argue. Oh, was Lieutenant de Witt—what's her name—OK'd for second doc?"

"Yes, and her husband for astrogator. Special permission came through. They both realize that it will probably be only one trip they'll have together."

"Memo—to OC Space College—meet me re organization astrogation training and recruitment; possible circulation of mathematics men in universities. I'll be told that it's not my business directly, but have a go. Next?"

"Panos' documents have arrived."

"Right. Next?"

"I'm all on my own tonight. My Ivan's on duty."

Said the admiral: "I think I'll get me a fifth of whisky, and retire to bed with it and the 'March of Space' omnibus edition on the vid."

"I ought to come over and console you," she suggested.

Damn, Carter thought, there's many a true word. He said, "You're too young. Now, if your mama was anywhere as good looking as her daughter—" He barked. "Pringle, stop wasting official time. Ring you tomorrow."

"Good luck," she said, "and watch the adjectives."

Her pert face faded from the screen. "There she goes again," Carter growled to himself. "Where the hell does she get that odd idea about the sort of man I am?"

Then he decided to phone a woman who *did* know what sort of a man he was. He would ring Velma, and she would talk of domestic nothings and of the children *and* the grandchildren. A good dose of that would stop the old hulk from drifting off into forbidden ports.

THUNDER OF STARS

We are concerned that too many earthmen seek for substitutes and reject reality, accept palliatives when they should demand cures, cling to lies instead of loving the truth. Against this great wrong, our faith earnestly desires to work with others of like mind.

(The Dalai Lama, guest of honor at the World Council of Buddhists, Rangoon. June 2161)

HELEN LINDSTROM stood at the "down" elevator of the seventh-level roll-road. The night was warm and humid, and sulkily grumbling thunderstorms were building up over the entire lakes area. North of her, she could see where the far lights over Michigan Water weaved, changed and flickered, blotted out irregularly by the steel and concrete towers of the great conurbation. Traffic hummed and throbbed above and below her. People passed on the roll-road, laughing and talking; somewhere nearby a drunk was singing tunelessly. A police hovervan droned over, its red and green lights flashing steadily.

She had thought, when the day's session was over, that she would stay in the hotel, eat, read and maybe see a show, then go to bed. But those final minutes alone in the monitor room with Tom Bruce had shattered her already crumbling illusion of composure. Now she knew that what she had really been waiting for was some gesture, some indication from him, so that she could, without a complete sacrifice of all self-respect, go to him. Any other plans had been a sop to her pride which would have been readily abandoned. But his gesture had not been the one she had hoped for. His cold anger had only served to confirm his rejection of her, and she was once more alone.

She opened her shoulder bag, took out a slim cigar and lit it. She was coming to need tobacco. What would be next, she wondered, alcohol, drugs? And with the thought, the gaunt face with its clownishly inept makeup loomed again in her mind. Sarah Baker, in the manner of her dying, had come to live forever with Helen Lindstrom. Moving quickly, in an effort to shake off the encroaching associations of remorse and fear, she stepped into the lift, which took her down to the pleasure grounds of the Little Loop.

Down in the lower levels there were no roll-roads, and pedestrians only were allowed. Police patrolled discreetly and only interfered in cases of violence, which, even including plain, ordinary mugging, were not very common. There was no telling who these people were, or what was their occupation; they wore bright, off-duty clothes, and their purpose was pleasure. Helen strolled casually along a street lined on either side with bars and restaurants.

"Hey!" A man's voice came from close behind her. "In a hurry?"

She ignored the clumsy pick-up attempt, refusing to be drawn out of her determined relaxation.

"You with the orange pants ..." It was a big-sounding voice, and he was nearer.

A hand stroked her buttock.

Damn the fool! Why couldn't he see that she wanted to be left alone?

The hand slipped round her waist.

Almost without conscious thought, her trained body moved into self-protective action. Grabbing at the wrist, she dragged the man forward, off-balance and gasping his surprise. He was thick-set, close cropped, with a snarling bully's face.

"Hey!"

She twisted the arm as he lurched past, shifted grip and braced herself, bringing his forearm across her thigh. The man screamed as his limb snapped like a rotten branch, and he rolled to the sidewalk, yelping in pain and fury.

Shocked by her own reflex violence, she turned and began to walk away.

"Just a minute!"

She stopped and turned. The police patrolman was small and springy, unobtrusively loaded with telecoms gear and small armament. "Yes?"

"This way." He led her back to where a small crowd was gathered round the injured man. "Now, how did this happen?"

A brown, flat-nosed man in bright blue, with a flower in his thick fuzzy hair said: "I saw it, patrolman. Self-defense. Assault on the person. She's clear."

The patrolman addressed Helen. "Is that so?"

She nodded. "He couldn't keep his hands to himself."

"He will now, for a while," the patrolman said. "Right. I'll accept the self-defense plea." He spoke the details into his hand recorder. "But there has been an injury, so I'll need names. Card, please, witness."

The fuzzy-haired man passed over his identity card, and the patrolman read it. The crowd, seeing that this was routine sidewalk justice, began to melt away. The injured man lay quiet now, his eyes staring their impotent hate at Helen.

The patrolman passed back the card of the witness and spoke politely to Helen. "Yours, please?"

She produced it. On the outside it was no different from anyone else's. The patrolman looked at it, then sharply back at her. Then he read it again, and handed it back.

"O.K., ma'am. I'll remember that. Put it on record later." He saluted, then pressed a button on his communicator and called medical services.

"Thank you, patrolman." She turned and walked on along the sidewalk, eager to get away from the scene of the encounter and the curious eyes that still studied her. She felt sorry for the man whose arm she had broken, but he had asked for it. Perhaps he would be more careful next time.

She quickened her pace, hurrying along through thronged, garishly lighted streets, past bars, dance shows, strip joints, gambling clubs, each offering their own particular brand of oblivion or excitement. It seemed to her, as she walked, that the ghost of Sarah Baker sat firmly on her shoulders, whispering to her of her own loneliness, of the barren life that lay ahead of her as an officer of the Corps.

She stopped at a wide intersection, joining a crowd who were watching a wiry brown man, clad only in a scrap of lastex, performing adagio acrobatics with two girls similarly exposed. She stood and watched the tirelessly graceful trio.

"They do it for kicks," said a voice at her elbow. "They're all three computer programmers, but they come here every fine Tuesday in the summer. Compensatory activity, I suppose."

The speaker was the little patrolman. He was disposed to be helpful. "They got that guy to the hospital, ma'am."

"Good. Thanks for what you did."

"Nothing. Just one point, ma'am . . ."

"Yes?"

"I don't want any trouble on my patch."

She found herself liking this earnest, obviously sincere little man. "Do you think I'm going to make trouble?" she said, smiling.

"No, of course not, not you." He was respectful, even slightly embarrassed. "But—well, you noticed I just remembered your name and number, to put it on tape later?"

"I see . . ."

"You're a striking looking person ma'am. Like, you don't take what *you've* got off with a uniform. I mean, you just *are* noticeable. There have been a lot of pictures in the papers, and on TV."

"As far as I can tell, you're the only person who's recognized me so far," she said.

"Maybe so, but there's a lot of feeling stirred up by this inquiry . . ." He looked at her pleadingly.

"Thanks, I appreciate your concern," she said warmly. "But tonight is just one time when I don't feel like sitting on my own in a hotel room. I'm sorry. And thanks again."

She walked on her way.

Turning a corner, she found a bar. Inside, the atmosphere was good and normal. The lights were soft, and there were two live musicians playing old Spanish music on guitars. One of them announced their next piece: "Zapateado de las Campañas."

She sat at a corner table and ordered a large bourbon. When it came, she drank it quickly and ordered another, not because she wanted to get drunk rapidly, but because she wanted peace and a stilling of the voices that nagged inside her head.

When the musicians finished she applauded and

made a request: " 'Recuerdos de la Alhambra,' por favor?"

The musicians were delighted. Among a mass of indifferent philistines, they had found an *aficionada.* They beamed at her and prepared to play again.

They never got to it.

As the guitarists were discussing a fine point of tuning, a thin figure in gray coveralls suddenly appeared in front of her table.

"Show me your face," he demanded.

She looked up, startled, into an emaciated visage whose principle feature was a pair of burning, intense eyes.

"Your name's Lindstrom!"

She stood up, and found that she matched him in height. "Yes?"

"You killed my brother—you and that murderous bastard Bruce!" The too-bright, hot eyes remained on her as he called: "Jovanka, here's one of them! Laszlo—here!"

A man and a woman, poorly dressed, grim of face, left another table and came toward her.

"Yes, she's the one. I seen a hundred pictures of her," said the second man.

"Haughty bitch!" the woman said quietly. "I'll tear her guts out!"

The first man kept looking at Helen with his mad eyes. Still looking, he flung away the table which separated them and aimed a brutal kick at her stomach.

Helen caught the foot as it rose. It was almost too easy. Pulling on the foot, she sent the man bowling backward. The woman came forward with a bottle and threw it. Helen ducked, and it shattered against the wall behind her. The second man swore and sprang forward, aiming a blow at her chin. She rolled back to avoid it and slipped.

As she fell, her head struck the edge of a chair. Her senses reeled, but she did not lose consciousness. She stayed on her hands and knees, shaking her head, aware of a pandemonium of shouts and screams around her, thinking vaguely that maybe this was what she had come here for, deliberately to offer herself for punishment so that she could in some manner exorcise the guilt that plagued her.

An enormously powerful arm came round her waist and lifted her to her feet. She remained limp, docile as an animal about to be slaughtered, as she waited for the blow to fall. But no blow came. She was dumped into a chair. Blinking, shaking her head, she gazed around her. The men and the woman who had attacked her were lying on the floor unconscious. The other customers in the bar stood watching as a big man talked into a communicator.

It was Sharva.

He finished talking into the instrument and came to her.

"You all right?"

"A bit dizzy." She managed to focus more steadily on the three figures on the floor. "What did you do?"

"Three pots from a riot dart gun, that's all. I've called the local patrol."

"*You* called them?"

"I'm a Senior Lieutenant of the JAG's department. That also makes me a policeman, remember?"

She nodded at him shakily. "Whatever you are, thank God you turned up when you did."

A voice was saying: "Come on, people, let's ignore it. The police have it in hand. Pepe, Raoul, how about some more music?"

Sharva said: "You seemed to be doing pretty well, but I figured you wouldn't want to go on handling three of them on your own. The woman had a knife, by the way."

She shivered slightly.

"You called me, sir?" The little patrolman appeared, slightly breathless. He saw Helen. "Huh. Remember what I said, ma'am?"

Helen raised one hand and essayed a shaky smile. "And you were so right, patrolman."

"I'd rather have been wrong. You've spoilt a quiet night," the patrolman said, as he took Sharva's card. He inspected it and returned it with deference. "Yes, sir. If you'll call in and record a statement before ten hours tomorrow morning, that should cover it." He nodded toward the drugged figures on the floor. "I'll call the wagon for these three. I'm booking them on a charge of unprovoked assault; well, that's what we shall call it." His keen face looked disapprovingly at Helen. "Commander Lindstrom, why don't you let the Lieutenant take you home?"

"Yes, I think that's a good idea," Sharva said. Slipping his strong arm under her elbow, he helped Helen to her feet.

"I'm all right," she said, embarrassed in the unaccustomed role, but aware in the face of his controlled strength that she really was the weaker.

They both said good night to the patrolman, and walked out of the bar.

"There's an elevator just around the corner," Sharva said. "Once we're up on the seventh we can take a cab."

His strong hand on her arm was a comfort as they walked along the street. The colored lights, the crowds, seemed to have lost their carnival gaiety now. She shivered, moving close to his big body.

"Those three . . . they would have gladly torn me to pieces," she said. "The inquiry—all that talk and argument means nothing beside that kind of feeling, does it?"

"It will, once the truth is established," Sharva said. "Then they will have to accept, and forget their grief." He looked down at her as they waited for the elevator. "Why didn't you stay at the hotel? If you wanted to get plastered, you could have done it there in safety."

"I . . . wanted to go out. To be free of uniform and what uniform means."

He nodded his large head slowly. The red trousers and black shirt seemed exactly the right colors for him. She could smell that he liked a mixture of pine plus something slightly more acrid in his bath. Tom Bruce was a big man, but Sharva was not far short of enormous. Yet there wasn't an ounce of surplus flesh on him, and his movements had the suppleness of some dark jungle cat.

"*You* came out," she said.

"I'm on a jag, too."

"Drinking?"

He suddenly looked boyish and shamefaced. "No. I'm a glutton for the old re-created arts exhibitions and concerts. I've been getting high on a concert of twentieth-century Negro music."

"Your secret passion," she said, smiling up at him. She suspected that here was the first truly integrated, civilized human being she had met in years. Perhaps it was the fact that Sharva, despite his commission in the Corps, was still basically a lawyer rather than an operational officer, but she had the feeling that there would always be room in his world for unashamed individuality and human feeling.

"I don't want to go back to the hotel," she said.

He surveyed her with concern. "You mustn't stay around here, Lieutenant Commander; it would be too dangerous."

She frowned and pleaded gently. "No ranks. Call me Helen. What's your name?"

"Paul." He smiled slowly.

"You have anything special arranged for tonight, Paul?" she said, as the elevator arrived and shed its load of passengers.

He took her arm with gentle firmness. "I do now," he said.

They got off the elevator at the fourth level. Here the prices were higher, and the types of entertainment offered were more discreet. He was a considerate, knowledgeable escort who sensed that, for tonight at least, she preferred to be relieved of all burden of choice, content to be simply a woman, and eager to forget that she was anything else.

Eventually, in a restaurant that was an indoor garden with whispering fountains and soft lighting, they sat and ate Japanese food. She drank sake, but he would have only water.

"Feel better?"

"Fine, thank you." Her face clouded. "But I'm not looking forward to tomorrow. That inquiry . . . I hate it, hate even thinking about it."

He put his big hand over hers. "You're not to worry. If you worry, you make my job harder."

"It *is* going to go right, isn't it, Paul?" She was begging for reassurance.

"I think so," he said soberly. "Morton makes a lot of noise, but the truth must be established in the long run."

"The truth," she echoed bleakly. "What is the truth?"

"That you and Bruce did what had to be done."

"But did we?" The conflicting, kaleidoscopic pattern rushed back into her mind, breaking down the temporary calmness. "What if my calculations were wrong?

It all happened so quickly, I could have made a mistake . . ."

"No!" he said firmly. "You're not even to think that to yourself, because, if you think it, when Morton gets you on the witness stand he'll have you saying it. You must stick completely, without wavering, to the letter of Commander Bruce's report."

"My Commander, right or wrong?"

"Your Commander *right*," he said. "And now, we shall stop this and talk about something else. Where do you come from?"

Oh, it felt good to be told so firmly what to do; to know that this man understood and to accept what he said with a childlike faith. "Stockholm," she said. "And you?"

"Teheran." He began to talk, telling her of his early life, sharing memories of small, everyday things in such a way that they became precious for her also. He was a good, almost hypnotic storyteller, with all the feeling for narrative of his ancient people, and she allowed herself to be soothed by his voice and by the sake.

She was looking at Paul Sharva and thinking of Tom Bruce, at first. But not much later she was thinking of Paul Sharva alone and thinking how a man like this could fill and enrich her life, how with him she could be a real woman. The practical side of her nature warned her that such a relationship was not for her, but even so, there could be no harm in . . .

"Would you care for a temporary attachment?" she said, coming to a sudden decision.

He smiled with genuine pleasure. "I'm honored to be asked. Naturally, I've been admiring you."

"Why naturally? I may not be the type that arouses anything in you. Then it would be a poor performance. For all I know, you may like small, plump dark women—Persian types."

"Oh, no, it doesn't follow at all."

"No affection, Paul. Just satisfaction. Tell me how you want it, and I'll tell you my needs. Agreed?"

"Of course." His smile was gentle. "I understand. Shall we go?"

When they got back to the Oppenheimer Hotel, she said in the elevator. "My room or yours?"

"I have a double bed in mine."

"You prepared for visitors?"

"No. I sprawl somewhat."

"Yours, then."

The door closed behind them and they were in another world—*his* world. The colors of the room were gold and black, the furnishings almost without ornament.

He came and stood behind her, putting his arms round her, strong yet gentle. She closed her eyes as the male perfume of his body enveloped her, and relaxed.

"Did you change your mind about me?" he asked softly.

"From when to when?" she asked, not understanding.

"You were pretty stand-offish the first time we met."

"I was . . . worried."

"Oh. About the—" He stopped short. "Tonight we're not talking about that, or worrying." He turned her round to face him and showed big, even white teeth in a smile. "You care for a drink? I don't, as you know, but . . ."

She drew him to her. "I didn't come for a drink, Paul."

He kissed her, and drew a hand along her thigh. The touch was charged by the growing desire of both their bodies. He released her and said: "I'll make it a shower. Not long." He went into the bathroom and a few moments later the hiss of water was audible.

She was already naked save for the band round her hair, when he called from the shower: "Are you coming in?"

She walked in. "I'm here."

He stuck his head out of the jets, staring in admiration as the water made seaweed tracks in the hair of his hard brown body. "Allah's eyes! You're so big, and so beautiful. All cream and gold."

She stood smiling at him. "I think you're kind of beautiful, too."

"A hairy ape man, you mean." He laughed. "How can such an object be beautiful?"

"That depends on who's looking, doesn't it?" she said.

Everything about him was over-scale; but could he, would he be right for her? She had become so used to Tom Bruce. Everything had to be rediscovered, readjusted, with someone new. If Paul Sharva was too quick, or too selfish, it would be worse than deprivation. She thrust aside her doubts and stepped into the shower with him.

His hands trembled as he took hold of her. They kissed, gently at first, then fiercely, as the water caressed their bodies. She pressed hard to him, took a handful of his thick hair, grasping it tightly.

"You're on fire," he said, and his voice was not steady.

"What did you expect?" She stepped out of the shower and stood in front of the drying jets of warm air. "Keep your hands *on* me, Paul. I want your hands *on* me, *on* me."

She turned toward him, the warm air making a halo of her golden hair. Placing her hands on his dark chest, she ran them down slowly, caressing, down past his ribs, his hard, flat belly until the fingers met, intertwining, and she felt the throbbing strength of him.

"Come into me now—now!" she whispered, releasing him and moving from the bathroom.

"No play . . . ?"

She turned and held out her arms.

"Not this time," she panted, lips drawn back from her teeth. "Later, later. I want you *now*!"

"You *are* afraid I shall be too quick," he said.

"Don't talk!" She pulled back the covers of the bed.

Her hard nipples burrowed into the thick, black hair of his chest. He smelled good and fresh; he controlled a rhythm that was growing steadily faster. Soon his expertise took control of her, and she began to clutch at his back, as she strove to devour more and more of him. She felt his teeth in the flesh of her shoulder, and the pain gave her the final thrust she needed. She held on with all her strength, and then they reached the climax together.

The warmth that flooded through her was marred only by a passing thought: "a few more times, and it would be as good as with Tom . . ."

"No, no," she said. "Don't leave me, yet. Stay where you are, just for a few minutes."

He nodded, panting, and smiled. "Did I hurt you?"

"Where?"

"Your shoulder."

"Oh. No, not really. Any blood?"

"Bruise. Sorry."

"Don't be. I think it helped." She looked up at him, drawing a hand down his dark jowl. "That was good, very good."

"I'm glad. I was a bit nervous . . . so much I didn't know about you."

"You knew enough." Gratitude for the relief of their first encounter flooded through her, making her forget future troubles.

There, in the softly lit, black-and-gold warmth, they lay side by side.

He said: "Couldn't this go on longer?"

"Past tonight?"

"Why not?" He raised on one elbow. "No strings—I understand that. But . . . well, if I'm good for you, you'd be good for me. I'm an obsessionist. I work hard, and my hobby's mostly my work. I could . . . well, be around whenever you wanted me?"

She felt a slight pang. He was being humble. A man such as he shouldn't be humble, unless it was because, in taking the job he had, he was inspired by an ideal of service to his fellows. But humble here, with her . . . She stopped her thoughts. She wanted a man for now, for a few nights, not for the future. There was no forever in this, no future, just a night-to-night present. And he was the man she wanted.

"That's a bargain," she said.

He was running his hands over her body. Though he had satisfied her well, she knew that she would want him again, very soon.

"Is that a bruise?" He had his hand on her stomach.

She had forgotten, for a moment. Then she remembered. "Yes."

"How did you do it?"

"I had a quarrel with an anti-grav lift."

"Hm? Oh, *that* lift. Yes, I saw it on the news."

"I didn't. It must have looked comic."

"Taken with a hand recorder. It looked very brave."

It was a death wish, she thought. But only Sarah Baker was killed. Poor Sarah Baker.

She said: "I didn't think what I was doing. Otherwise I might have walked away." She stretched and turned toward him. "Paul, do you snore as well as sprawl?"

"You'd better stay and find out."

"This court is prepared to accept your conclusions, Professor," Alote Jones said. "On the understanding that you are prepared to supply copies of your calculations for expert examination later."

"Naturally, Your Honor," Bergman said.

"Then please continue."

"Briefly, the situation was this. The Space Corps experts have already explained that since the *Athena*'s engines had been destroyed, the ship was capable of neither acceleration nor deceleration. This much must be obvious, even to a layman. However, the Corps appear to have made a further assumption which is not strictly true, namely, that the ship would have continued to follow precisely the same course vector. I have examined the positions of the various planetary bodies of the solar system at the time of the incident in relationship to this predicted course, and it is my belief that the Space Corps calculations do not give sufficient consideration to the fact that *Athena*'s course vector would have passed through the orbit of Mars, and the gravitic attraction of Mars would undoubtedly have been sufficient at that distance to pull *Athena* off course. The figure of two thousand miles is, of course, an approximate one, but the ship would certainly *not* have been on collision course with Earth."

Lieutenant Sharva rose to his feet. "Your Honor, in a theoretical argument of this nature it is very possible for experts to hold, quite sincerely, differing opinions. The information available at the time pointed quite clearly, in the opinion of Corps tracking stations, to the conclusion that *Athena* would crash into Earth, with disastrous results. I would beg you to appreciate the pressure of time involved."

Morton countered sharply. "Your Honor, it would seem the Lieutenant is trying to tell us that, although the Space Corps was in possession of insufficient data to be certain that *Athena* was on collision orbit with Earth, Commander Bruce nevertheless made his decision to destroy the ship and five hundred people."

"The judiciary is quite capable of making its own interpretations," Alote Jones said severely. "We thank you for your assistance in this matter, Professor Bergman, and would be obliged if you would hold yourself available for consultation at a later stage."

Bergman stepped down from the witness stand, bowed to the judiciary and made his exit.

"Your Honor, might I make a request?" Morton was on his feet again, sharp, like a hound smelling blood. "We have heard a great deal of technical evidence in this matter, but Commander Bruce is, so far, only known to us as a face on a teletape screen. Surely the time is now ripe when we should have the opportunity to meet him in person and make some assessment of his character and record?"

Sharva rose. "Your Honor, I cannot see that any practical purpose would be served by placing Commander Bruce on the stand at this stage."

"Please be seated, Lieutenant Sharva," Alote Jones said severely. "Commander Bruce has been subjected to a great deal of adverse publicity already, wild accusations have been thrown at him and allegations of incompetence have been made. Under the circumstances, I feel sure that he would welcome the opportunity of putting his point of view. There will now be a recess of one and a half hours, after which we shall call Commander Bruce to the witness stand for questioning."

THUNDER OF STARS

I said a prayer with the president on moonbase. It was not just for him—it was for everybody, everywhere. I thought about those words and I know that they could even include people—creatures, perhaps—we haven't yet met. Homo sapiens can't be the only species with the keys of the Kingdom.

(Lt. William Kibbee, Space Corps Chaplain, in a TV interview.)

WHEN THE court reassembled after the break, its atmosphere was one of brooding, unnatural quiet. Bruce took his place on the witness stand. His face was an uncompromising, stern mask, he stood rigidly to attention as the judiciary filed in and took their places.

Judge Alote Jones surveyed the court with quiet severity for a whole minute, then he addressed the witness.

"Lieutenant Commander Bruce, the court would be obliged if you could now give us a more personal account of the events which led up to the ... er ... encounter with the *Athena*."

"Encounter" might have been a word chosen to sting one man in the public gallery to the roots of his being. His shout traveled perfectly in the fine acoustics of the hall.

"Encounter? Encounter? Say what you mean! He

killed them, every last one of them, the bloody, stiff-necked murderer!"

The shout was a sudden shower of sparks, dropped into the powder keg of brooding quiet. Sound erupted like an explosion, a wave of explosions, like a hurricane sea thundering against the breakwaters of sanity. The pandemonium roared from a thousand throats; the raging public gallery was its center. Men and women stood and screamed, stamped and wept. They called the names of their lost ones, hurled imprecations at the judge and judiciary, at the name of the Space Corps, at God, Buddha and Mohammed, but most of all they concentrated their ferocity on one, hated, single syllable—Bruce—and the man who bore that name.

There was no need for the TV cameras to seek dramatic pieces of action and come close to them; every inch of the public gallery was filled with anger and suffering, every member, almost without exception, was baying for blood, for the blood of the man upon whom the blame could be set and from whom vengeance could be exacted. Howling through the hall, overloading microphones and amplifiers, the crescendo of rage and frustration beat against the ears of listeners like blows from a club. Throughout the solar system billions of watchers stared at their screens and shuddered at the terrible, ravening power of human anger.

At the center of the storm Tom Bruce stood, gazing neither to right nor to left. His refusal to acknowledge the fury that surrounded him served only to further enrage the mob.

Alote Jones rested his arms on the bench in front of him, linked his fingers, and stared with black impassivity at the public gallery where the security men waited for the signal to go to work. The whole area could have been hazed down to somnolence with Pax capsules in less than three minutes. Security men and judiciary expected the judge to signal.

But he did not signal. He sat and listened to the raging while cameras recorded and transmitted the scene, while commentators said nothing because there was nothing their words could add. The only action the security men on the balcony took was the forcible retention of a woman who, streaming with tears and moaning like an injured animal, attempted to throw herself from the edge to the floor below.

Gradually, those who thought they were taking action found that there was no reaction, and with the first frenzy of release past, they began to wonder why. Gradually the sound began to decrease.

Judge Alote Jones waited. At least there was a kind of silence, an ashamed, uneasy hush, broken by small moans and sobbings; the reaction of a hysterical, abominably behaved child, brought to the point of exhaustion by its own tantrums and beginning to be fearful of retribution.

Judge Alote Jones pressed a button on his bench and spoke into a microphone. His voice was audible to the entire court. "Recordist? Play that back to them, at full volume," he ordered.

There were gasps of alarm.

"No one may leave this court," ordered the Judge. "Just stay where you are and listen."

The sound system burst into life, and the occupants of the hall suffered the noise again with all its bestiality and horror. It raged on and on, seemingly without end, and then, at last, it stopped. When it was done, the creators of the disturbance looked down at the floor, or at the ceiling, not ever at one another.

"And now," Judge Jones said calmly, "perhaps we can continue. Commander Bruce?"

"Your Honor." Bruce inclined his head slightly, then

told his story, beginning from the moment that Perimeter Station Fifteen notified the appearance of the UFO. The court listened in silence to the cool, emotionless voice, and heard him out.

"Thank you, Commander Bruce," Alote Jones said when the tragic story was concluded. "Do you wish to make any comment on the theories of Professor Bergman?"

Bruce's back was ramrod straight, his green eyes unblinking as he stared at the Judge. "Your Honor, I made my decision on the basis of the facts available to me and I took action accordingly."

"And you have had no second thoughts?"

The lines at the corners of Bruce's mouth deepened. "Why would I have second thoughts?" he demanded.

Helen Lindstrom, watching his uncompromising face on the monitor screen, raised her palms to her temples. "God, what arrogance! Why can't he bend, just a little?"

"Because he's a Corps officer, and because he's *right*," said Junius Carter, who was sitting beside her. "Why *should* he crawl to these damned civilians?"

She looked at the stocky body and the wrinkled, implacable face of Carter. "Because for one thing, it is taxes, levied on those civilians, that maintain the Space Corps. Maybe it's time for the Corps to begin taking lessons in humility."

"To hell with that!" growled Carter. "Pipsqueaks like Morton can yell their heads off all they like. They'll not touch the Corps while we have the President's backing."

Helen said: "But what if something were to happen to him, as it very easily could, at his age? How do you know that the next President would be as sympathetic to the Corps?"

Carter scowled. "It's probably a good thing for us all that you're not the one out there on the witness stand."

Helen met his gaze steadily. They were two of a kind, this man and Tom Bruce. These were the true officers of the Space Corps, the men of whom it could be said, with justification, that they were "All Corps." And with this recognition came the growing certainty that this was a way she could never be.

"I think you're right, Admiral," she said quietly, while inside her head a voice demanded: "Who? What am I?"

Admiral Carter grunted and turned his attention back to the screen.

Morton was examining Bruce. His confidence was unshaken.

"Lieutenant Commander Bruce, how long have you been an officer of Space Corps?"

"Fifteen years."

"And I believe that during your three years at Sandpoint you were awarded the Star of Honor?"

"That is true."

"Commander Bruce, would you explain to the court the nature of this decoration?"

Bruce frowned. "The Star of Honor is a mark of distinction awarded to the officer cadet with the highest grades in all subjects throughout the course."

"A distinction which was gained also by a member of the present judiciary, Rear Admiral Mariano," Morton said, bowing slightly in the direction of the bench.

"That is true."

"In fact, Commander Bruce, it could be said that the award of the Star of Honor is usually an indication that the holder is likely to go fast and far in the matter of promotion in the Corps. I cite, once again, the distinguished career of Admiral Mariano, who is, I understand, two years your junior."

"There are other factors . . ."

"Then you don't find it strange that, in sixteen years of service with the Corps, you have failed to attain a rank higher than Lieutenant Commander?"

"Not really," Bruce said calmly. "Promotion in the Space Corps is not an automatic procedure."

"But an officer of your capability, of your record?"

"I run System Patrol, and the establishment for that job calls for a CO with the rank of Lieutenant Commander."

"Mr. Morton," the Judge said, "be plain."

Morton inclined his head. "Very well, Your Honor. I *will* be plain." He turned and motioned to his assistant, who rose and walked toward the bench, carrying a sheaf of documents. "I would like to offer these Fax copies of a certain document in evidence."

Admiral Carter hunched forward, glaring at the screen. "What's the clever bastard up to now?" he demanded as Alote Jones examined the document and the court waited.

When the Judge looked up eventually, his dark features were grim. "I have in front of me a document which purports to be a Fax copy of a Space Corps Form D346, referring to Lieutenant Commander Bruce. May I ask where you obtained this document, Mr. Morton?"

"With due respect, Your Honor, I must reserve the right to protect my source of information at this time," Morton said.

"Your Honor!" Admiral Suvorov spoke aloud and clearly for the first time, from his place on the judiciary bench. "If this document is a genuine copy, I object most strongly to its being offered in evidence. Disclosure of classified information can only be against the general interest."

Judge Alote Jones nodded. "I take your point, Admiral Suvorov." He turned his attention to the Excelsior Corporation lawyer. "Mr. Morton, unless you are prepared to submit a detailed testimony as to how you obtained a copy of this confidential, internal Corps document, I cannot allow you to submit it for our consideration."

"That's shot him up his rear jets!" exclaimed Carter, gleefully. The camera zoomed in on the features of Morton.

Far from being perturbed by the Judge's rebuke, the lawyer's thin face held the suggestion of a self-satisfied smile. "Your Honor, copies of the document were distributed at my press conference during the midday recess. I understand that some of the earlier editions are already on the streets, carrying the full text."

"Mr. Morton, this is highly irregular!" Alote Jones said.

"Your Honor, I merely seek the complete truth."

Admirals Suvorov and Mariano had both left their seats at the bench and were moving toward the Judge's position. Grim faced, he waved them back. "I'm sorry, gentlemen, but if this matter has already been made public there is no point in denying its admission here."

The Admirals stopped and conferred together briefly. Then returned to their seats.

"Very well, Mr. Morton, continue," said Judge Jones.

"Thank you, Your Honor," Morton said. Returning to his table, he picked up a file. "And now, for the benefit of those who are not familiar with Space Corps procedure, I should explain that Form D346 is a standard Record sheet, such as is to be found in the personal file of each and every member of the Corps. On this form are entered the brief details of any charges and punishments incurred by the subject during his or her service. The particular Form D346 with which we are concerned here is one referring to the career of Lieutenant Commander Thomas Winford Bruce, the officer who now stands in the witness box. The entry to which I wish to draw the attention of this inquiry reads as follows:

" 'Charged 5/3/56 with exceeding the reasonable execution of his duty and with failing to report an emergency to his Commanding Officer. In that while in charge of a planetary landing party, this officer did willfully bring about the death of forty-one human colonists by summary execution, in the absence of any specific order from his commanding officer. (Complete details of the charge, and testimony offered to the Court Martial are retained in Maximum Security File PZ6753, under Section 254A of Space Corps Standing Orders.) A Court Martial presided over by Admiral Charles Norman, and held *In Camera*, found Lieutenant Bruce guilty. He was severely reprimanded and deprived of five years' seniority. Sentence confirmed by Presidential Order dated 23/7/56.' "

The court watched in shocked silence as Morton laid the file back on the table and turned to face the witness, who still stood, ramrod straight at attention.

"Lieutenant Commander Bruce, do you deny that this is a true extract from your personal file?" Morton said.

"I do not," replied Bruce.

"In that case, Commander, would you care to comment?"

"I am not at liberty to do so," Bruce said. He faced his questioner without apparent emotion.

"In that case, I will attempt an interpretation," Morton said with some relish. "We are not supplied with the name of the planet upon which these events took place, but it was quite clearly a colonial one. We are all aware that there have been, from time to time, certain differences between the Space Corps and the inhabitants of developing colonies. I cite, for instance, the uprising on Mafti Three, where there was a dispute between the local Space Corps commander and the democratically elected government of the colony."

Alote Jones intervened. "The Mafti Three case was heard before the Supreme Court five years ago and the findings of the court were in favor of the Space Corps action, which was taken to curb undesirable political developments in the administration of the colony."

Morton bowed his head in the direction of the judiciary. "Quite so, Your Honor. I was not suggesting that the planet referred to in this document *is* Mafti Three, but merely making a general observation that there have been a number of recorded instances of conflict between the Space Corps and colonists."

"Your Honor, I must protest!" Admiral Suvorov rose to his feet. "It is well known that in addition to its exploration and survey functions, the Corps is entrusted with police duties."

"The gallant Admiral's point is well taken," Morton said smoothly. "Perhaps he would like to tell us about this police action? Why were the details of this incident not made public at the time? Is this, perhaps, another example of the well-known solidarity of the Space Corps?" He pitched his voice higher. "I ask again, *why were these people killed*?"

The spectators maintained their uneasy silence.

Suvorov looked around the court, then back to the Judge. "Your Honor, this is neither the time nor the place to discuss this matter."

"Then when will be the time and where the place?" Morton's voice climbed in volume and pitch, dominating a growing murmuring from the public galleries. He turned, with a calculatedly histrionic gesture, and pointed to Bruce. "This man, at the time a mere junior officer of the Corps, took it upon himself to execute forty-one—I repeat, forty-one—human beings, without even bothering to consult his commanding officer. Why was this action taken? Was it perhaps in order to quell some revolt similar to the Mafti Three affair? Were these people massacred, to quote an ancient and barbaric precedent, 'to encourage the others'? If so, I say that this was nothing less than bloody, mass murder! And for this, Lieutenant Bruce was *reprimanded*?" He spat out the four syllables of the last word in an echoing blast.

"Murdering swine!" The shout from the gallery cut in on Morton's words, the scream of a damned soul in torment. Simultaneously a needle gun flashed and a sliver of metal whipped from behind the witness stand, three inches from Commander Bruce's head. He remained unmoving, standing to attention, as for the second time that afternoon pandemonium reigned in the courtroom. Now, more even than before, the mob, deliberately inflamed by Morton, was howling for *his* blood.

Somewhere in the center of the gallery a knot of security men closed in on the man with the needle gun, Pax gas pistols in their hands. The man, shouting in Italian, backed away to the very edge of the gallery, waving his gun, but unwilling to fire again in the face of such odds. People, screaming and shouting, scattered away from him; and then a well-placed gas pellet dropped him where he stood.

His fall was a signal for even further uproar, and from the judge's bench a scuffling was visible at the back of the hall as a posse of wild-eyed, desperate men fought to get past the uniformed guards, with the obvious intention of dragging Bruce from the witness stand.

"Get Commander Bruce off the stand!" Alote Jones used the full power of the PA system. "Guards! Emergency A orders are now in operation! Clear the court. This inquiry stands adjourned until further notice. The counselors will report to my chambers in one hour's time!"

Helen Lindstrom watched the monitor screen as four armed security guards escorted Tom Bruce from the witness stand, up onto the stage and away into the wings. Then she turned sickly toward her companion.

"That bastard! That dirty, conniving, shit-throwing bastard!" roared Admiral Carter. "He knew bloody well that Tom Bruce could not defend himself in open court! That case was a Corps matter, top secret! I'm going to go down to Corps Records, and when I find the sniveling sonofabitch who talked, I'm going to tear him apart with my bare hands!" He stormed toward the door of the small room.

Helen hurried to intercept him. "Admiral! Tell me one thing."

"Yes?" He stopped and glared up at her.

"Did Tom Bruce *really* kill those people?" she asked.

"Of *course* he did," growled Carter. "But that's not the point! Corps Security has been breached! Get out of my way, woman!" He thrust past her and flung open the door.

Not the point! Helen slumped into a chair; she sobbed. Forty-one human beings dead, on some godforsaken, unnamed planet, massacred by the man who had shared her bed a thousand times. She had known he was ruthless, but *this* . . .

"Oh, God!" she moaned. "What kind of men are these?" And she knew the answer. These are your brother officers, your Corps commander. If you can't stand what they are, should you be one of them?

She thought about Paul.

"I trust you understand that by coming here you are making a complete shambles of both political and Corps protocol?" Henry Fong's face had all the scrutability of a pale brown egg as he surveyed his visitor.

Paul Sharva, poised uneasily on the edge of a chair that looked inadequate for the task of holding his big body, frowned. "Mr. Secretary, while I may be an officer of the Space Corps, I am by training and instinct a lawyer. As such, I consider it my duty to defend my client to the best of my ability. This I am not allowed to do at the moment."

"You have discussed the situation with your superiors?" Fong inquired blandly.

"The Judge Advocate General is at the moment on extended leave, and according to his office, quite untraceable," Sharva said. He looked for enlightenment at the other, and received none.

Fong nodded.

Sharva rose to his feet, surrendering to the tensions of a body that demanded movement. He moved restlessly. "Mr. Secretary, I have just come from the Corps Admin Headquarters, where I am outranked by practically everybody except the clerks. I have spent two whole hours there in conference with a herd of Admirals, Rear-Admirals and assorted brass, not one of whom is prepared to make a decision or take any action in this very urgent matter; and every time I've tried to open my mouth I've been told to sit tight and say nothing."

"There are times when that can be very good advice Lieutenant Sharva," Fong said.

"But this is not one of them!" Sharva stopped his pacing and towered over the Secretary's desk. "Mr. Secretary, if I am to defend Commander Bruce when that inquiry resumes, I *must* be given the full facts. I understand that the Confidential File containing those facts is held in the strongroom of this building."

"Under the Presidential seal, Lieutenant; which can only be broken at the express order of the President himself."

"Or, at your discretion, as the President's personal secretary."

"Only in the most extreme circumstances."

"These *are* extreme circumstances!"

Fong placed the tips of his carefully manicured fingers together and looked calmly at the big, dark man who faced him. "Tell me, Lieutenant, what do you expect to find in this confidential file?" he asked.

"Evidence that will enable me to establish quite clearly that Commander Bruce is not the wanton murderer the Excelsior representative has alleged him to be."

"What if I were to tell you that Morton was right, that Bruce was in fact a murderer, and he did kill, or cause to be killed, forty-one colonists?"

"In punishment for which action he was *reprimanded*?" Sharva said. "There's more to it than that, Mr. Secretary."

"Yes, Lieutenant, there's a great deal more to it," said Fong. "But is was decided at the time that it would be against the general interest to publish the full facts."

"*Whose* decision, Mr. Secretary?"

"That of the President, in consultation with the Admirals of Space Corps," said Fong. "I might add that there have been times since then when the President has voiced to me certain doubts about the wisdom of that decision."

"Then surely, if he were conscious, he would agree to the release of the file?"

Fong placed his hands, palms downward, on the desk top and looked steadily up at Sharva. "I wonder, do we have the right to anticipate the thoughts of such a great man?"

"The file, Mr. Secretary . . . ?"

"So young, and so impatient." The beginnings of a smile creased Henry Fong's smooth face. "All right, Lieutenant, I'll make a bargain with you. I'll arrange for you to have a private room in this building where you can read the file and see the tapes that go with it. On one condition: when you've studied the information made available to you, you must come back to me and we'll talk again about whether or not you should make that information public knowledge."

"Thank you, Mr. Secretary," Sharva said. But, even as he agreed thankfully, he found himself thinking that there might be something in this for the President's secretary.

Henry Fong raised his hands from the desk. "No, Lieutenant, don't thank me now; you may wish to withdraw your gratitude later."

Sharva saluted and left.

Henry Fong knew that when that time came, some way had to be found, some new method of binding together the disparate elements that went to make up the empire of United Earth. He closed his eyes for a moment, in silent prayer to the Great Architect of the Universe that his judgment was a true one and that through the words and actions of two men, each of whom held duty and principle above all thoughts of self, United Earth would survive.

It was past midnight when he came to her room. She rose from her sleepless bed, flinging on a negligee, and opened the door for him.

"Paul, where have you been? I've . . ." She stopped talking, immediately ashamed of her selfish preoccupation with her own agony, when she saw his face. His eyes held something beyond pain; they were the eyes of a man who had seen hell.

"Helen . . ." His arms reached out and pulled her close to him.

She yielded gladly, hungry for his affection. She sensed immediately that this was not the proud, animal sensuality they had known together on the previous evening, but a deeper, more spiritual need. They clung together like two children, each needing the security of the other's affection and warmth.

Later he undressed, showered and came back to her.

"Come and sleep," she said.

He laid his great head on her breast, and she held him, making small sounds of comfort, sensing his need, and feeling in this new, chaste relationship that she shared with him a greater love than she had ever experienced with any man. He was firstly her lover and then her child; she was strength to his weakness, yet knowing at the same time that this weakness was revealed to her alone because of his love and trust for her. She knew he had been hurt, deeply, and could not speak of it.

When he awoke, soon after dawn, the haunted look had gone from his eyes, as if sleep and her care had rationalized whatever had caused it. Fully awake, his face dark with morning stubble, he raised himself on one elbow and looked down at her.

"Thank you, Helen," he said. "Thank you for not asking for answers I can't give." He kissed her gently, then rose from the bed. "I have to go now," he said, buttoning the tunic of his uniform. "There's work, a great deal of work, to be done today."

"Can I help?"

He paused, looking down at her. "You have, already," he said gently.

"When shall I see you again?"

"If everything goes as I hope, this evening," he said. "Put some things in a bag, and I'll be here about eighteen hundred hours to collect you."

"We're going somewhere?"

He nodded. "The inquiry continues on Saturday, but tonight and tomorrow I want to be alone with you where we can forget it all."

"Can we do that?"

"Together . . . yes, we can," he said. "Now, I must go."

Admiral Sam Suvorov sighed as he picked a pile of accumulated papers from his IN tray and laid them on the desk in front of him. The vid buzzed. Suvorov's heart leapt as he reached for the switch. Perhaps this was the call he had been waiting for.

"Yes?"

"Presidential Secretary Fong is calling you, sir."

"All right, put him on."

"Good morning, Admiral Suvorov." The bland, brown features of Henry Fong appeared in the screen.

"Any news from Moon?" Suvorov asked immediately.

Fong shook his head slowly. "No, I'm afraid not. And when it does come there doesn't seem any likelihood that it will be favorable. According to Hurwitz, there's no will to live. Physically the operation was a success, but the mind has made its own decision to lay down its burden."

"Then there's no hope of a Presidential statement?"

"On the subject of the Pandora's box? No. However . . ."

Suvorov leaned forward tensely.

"Senior Lieutenant Sharva of the Judge Advocate General's Department is a determined young man," Henry Fong said unhurriedly.

"You've spoken to him?" Suvorov asked.

"At considerable length," replied Fong. "He came to see me yesterday afternoon."

"He had no authority! I'll have him—"

"Discharged from the Corps, I hope," Henry Fong said blandly. "I can use a man with Sharva's abilities in *my* department."

Suvorov glared at the slim, Buddha image of Henry Fong. *Damn the man*! Why couldn't he ever come right out and say what he meant? To add to his exasperation, he became aware of a commotion outside in his secretary's office. As he looked up, his door burst open and Rear Admiral Junius Carter appeared, trailed by an apologetic female sub-Lieutenant.

"What do you mean, he's *busy*?" roared Carter, his stubbly scalp bristling. "He can't be too busy to see *me*!"

The secretary retreated at a glance from Suvorov, closing the door behind her.

"Sit down and behave yourself, Junius!" commanded Suvorov. "I'm talking to the presidential secretary."

Carter grunted and subsided, simmering, into a chair that creaked underneath his bulk.

"The ubiquitous Admiral Carter, I presume?" Henry Fong said, making a steeple of his slim fingers. "I understand that the investigation of Corps Records was, shall we say, only a partial success?"

"I found the leak!" roared Carter, moving round into the range of the vidphone scanner.

"You found an unfortunate Petty Officer with a history of sexual . . . indiscretion, and scared him into taking a lethal dose of parathylide," Fong said. "Surely it would have been more constructive to have won the man's confidence with a view to finding out who was pressuring him?"

Carter looked uncomfortable. "I merely asked him a few simple questions."

"I can imagine," Fong said. "I would suggest that in future you stick to building spaceships and leave playing detective to those more suited to such work by temperament and training."

Admiral Suvorov ran the fingers of one hand through his thatch of gray hair. "Mr. Secretary, you were saying . . . about Lieutenant Sharva?"

"A good man, Admiral—without attempting to appear pious—a *good* man in most senses of the word—sincere, truthful, honorable, dedicated. Old-fashioned virtues, but not outmoded ones."

Suvorov frowned. "I'll admit, he's shown up well, so far . . ."

"Looks good on a television screen, too," said Henry Fong. "Solid, dependable, the kind of man people trust instinctively."

"So what do you want to do? Make a politician of him?" rumbled Junius Carter, who was becoming impatient.

"No, Junius, that's just what I don't want," Henry Fong said blandly. "Even if I thought he could be changed, I would want him just as he is."

"For what purpose?" asked Suvorov.

"I believe that such a man might be capable of presenting the facts of what happened on Minos IV in such a manner that he would win the unquestioning allegiance of his audience. In accordance with this belief, I have released into his keeping the Confidential File and all relevant data, assuring him that he has a completely free hand to handle the subject in any way he thinks fitting."

Both Admirals gaped at the smooth face on the screen.

"But surely that's a Presidential decision?" Suvorov said.

"Under normal circumstances, yes," Fong said. "But the President, as we all know, is not available."

"You mean you're going to let him go into open court and . . ." Carter's words trailed away as he tried to assess the implications of Fong's statement.

"Can you think of a better way of getting Commander Bruce *and the Corps* off the hook, at this particular time?" said Henry Fong. "And now, gentlemen, if you will excuse me, there is a great deal to be done." His face faded abruptly from the screen.

"Well I'll be damned!" Carter's face wrinkled in puzzlement. "Why the hell would Fong, after a lifetime safe on the sidelines, commit himself by making a decision like that?"

Suvorov regarded his companion soberly. "If I was in need of any confirmation that the President is dying, that was it," he said quietly.

"How's that?"

"Look at it this way, Junius. When Oharo dies, what happens?"

Carter shrugged. "Vice-President Wilkins takes over, I suppose."

"For the interim period, yes," Suvorov said. "But according to the constitution there has to be a Presidential election within three months, right? Fong is a patient man. He has been quite content to serve Oharo all these years; but now, make no mistake about it, he's done with self-effacement. I'll lay you a year's pay to a bag of peanuts that Fong is already making his preparations. And what candidate can possibly stand against him, with the readymade platform at his disposal? He's ex-right-hand man of the late, beloved President Oharo, able to pursue a continuity of policy. Tell me honestly,

Junius; who would you rather see in the Presidential chair, that nonentity Wilkins, or Henry Fong?"

"Well, if you put it that way, I suppose it's obvious," Carter said. "But I still . . ."

"Look, Junius, Fong knows all the angles, and all the right people. He'll make a damned good President," said Suvorov. "Something else he knows—that to be a strong, outward-looking President of United Earth, he needs the full backing of the Space Corps!"

A sudden animation fleshed out Carter's craggy features. "By God, you're right, Sam!" he roared. "Let's just hope Lieutenant Sharva is as good as Fong *thinks* he is."

THUNDER OF STARS

... But they are somewhere.
They have to be.
By all the laws of probability,
We should have met them before.
There, long before we reached the
   Rim, we should have found them.
Consider the odds.
We cannot be the only men....

(KILROY : I Kavanin.)

THE LAKE was in Northern Ontario, a sapphire between slopes of tumbled gray-brown rock topped with pines. There was a small beach made of transported sand, and a two-room wooden cabin sixty meters up the slope. The only neighbors were a pair of friendly squirrels and a few hundred water birds.

Paul Sharva stroked the length of her golden back. "You're sure you're not burning?"

Helen was lying, completely relaxed, her head cradled in her arms. "No, I had a light tan before."

Paul squinted up at the strong, morning sun. "Maybe, but a drop of this might help." He squeezed a colorless ointment out of a tube and began to apply it, working with loving care.

Drowsy and content as a stroked cat, she said: "The hire of all this must have cost you a packet."

"I have a friend in the business. But total exclusivity does come a little high."

"And all for yourself. Somewhere to think."

"Uh-uh."

"I think everyone should have a private lake, for thinking."

"And for fishing. But then, my kind of fishing just amounts to sitting and thinking." He was stroking her peachlike behind. "Mustn't miss this or you won't be able to sit down."

She wriggled gently. "How to make love with suntan lotion."

"What?"

"That's what you're doing, isn't it?"

"So?"

"So go on doing it."

He went on doing it, down her buttocks, the back of her thighs and calves. "Now turn over . . . Hey! Don't knock your communicator down."

She turned over and lay smiling up at him. "Damn my communicator. I only brought it to salve my conscience for goofing off like this. I'm sure the Corps can get along without me for one day, at least."

"At least," he repeated as he began to work down her neck and shoulders.

She reacted with sensuous pleasure to his light touch, as he spread the protective film over her breasts. "Mmm . . . Aren't we all bloody egoists?"

"Are we?" He spoke quietly, deliberately, as though words were valuable.

"Yes. I mean . . . look at the attention I'm getting."

"It's no more than you deserve. Besides, skin like yours, in this sun . . ."

She laughed. "That's a lawyer's trick, pretending to misunderstand so as to sustain a line of thought."

"Your perspicacity does you credit, ma'am." His hand stopped just above her navel. "In the sunlight that bruise looks a beauty. Any pain?"

"You're smoothing it away."

"We try to give satisfaction." He continued with the gentle spreading of the lotion.

"When you've finished me, I'll do the same for you," she said.

He laughed. "Me? All hair and mahogany?" He went on stroking; then he stopped. "I *do* need protection, but not against the sun."

She raised herself on one elbow. "Then against what?"

"Oh . . . To many people I'm the lone Persian bull who walks by himself. They find me efficient—which I am—and they find me spare on words; I'm that too, to most people."

"But not to me."

He regarded her seriously. "I'm glad you've got that point. I have solitary hobbies, because . . . well, because I'm that sort. I can fence myself in and get on with life better that way. But it doesn't mean that I don't want anyone inside the fence with me. Time for thinking, yes, but you can do your thinking *with* somebody if you find the right person."

"You mean that being with such a person can be as good as being alone, but better?"

He laughed. "And I never knew before that Lindstrom was an Irish name. Yes, that's exactly what I mean."

"Any religion, Paul?"

"My own mixture. A revision of Mohammedanism, plus my own bits of ancestor worship. It seems to work."

"I'm envious."

"Why?"

"Oh well, I suppose because you know where you fit in. You've organized yourself, looked right inside and said, 'This I ought to do, and this, and this.' And you've done it. You run life on *your* terms, don't you?"

"Pretty well, with some outstanding exceptions."

"Exceptions?"

"One, really. Before three nights ago, there were none."

She understood him perfectly. The summer morning suddenly became unbearably beautiful. Why didn't he have a wife and a family already? Because he was choosy, because he set a high valuation on love as opposed to making love. "And now there's me?"

"Yes." His answer was level, quiet, a statement of unchangeable fact and resolution.

It was what she had wanted to hear. She lay back again and closed her eyes. She felt his hand cup her breast, felt his thumb and finger caress a nipple. Then his hand patted her gently.

He said: "Closing your eyes won't make it go away."

"Shall we go up to the cabin?"

"That's no answer."

"There isn't supposed to be an answer. I enjoy you, and you enjoy me." She looked up at him sharply. "Don't you?"

"You don't have to ask that."

"Then what more do you want?"

"The *real* thing," he said seriously. "When we have each other it's wonderful, but the mating is for enjoyment only. In time, surely you understand that even such joy can become meaningless if it is without purpose?"

Her hands were on his shoulders, feeling the firm muscle beneath the dark skin. "You're a strange one, Paul," she murmured.

"Is it so strange to long for the day when you lie there, quietly, letting what I give you do the work it should?"

She trembled, as everything that was woman inside her surged upward in a torrent that responded to the longing of this man. This was what she wanted, too. Perhaps it was what she had been created for. "Paul . . ."

He covered her mouth with his gentle, big hand. "Helen, I want a wife—you."

She was seeking now for defenses and finding precious few. "My career . . ."

"I'll give you a career. Six sons. Wouldn't that be a career? You could sign out of the Corps."

"It's too late, Paul, years too late." She moved from him and sat with her hands clasped about her knees, aware of the stinging of unshed tears in her eyes.

"Helen, how can you be sad at what I've said?"

"Because some fools can be unhappy, even in heaven," she said, deliberately looking away from him. "Paul, how can someone as intelligent as you ask such a simple question?"

"The simplest ones are sometimes the hardest to answer," he said. "Don't make a decision now, just tell me you'll think about it."

"Are you *sure*, Paul?"

"I know the career for you, with the right man. And I'm the right man because I love you."

"You must be a rotten lawyer," she said softly. "You're so damned honest. I believe you think you mean it. But how can you know it's true?" She slapped a golden thigh. "It's not a bad body, Paul. It knows how to give as well as receive. That shows, even when I'm wearing uniform. Couldn't it be just that?"

"Remember the first time we met, in Patrols HQ? The mask of efficiency didn't work for me; your eyes showed me that you were unhappy, and I wanted to know what that unhappiness was . . . and what I could do about it."

She looked at his serious face and knew that he understood.

Judge Alote Jones took his seat at the bench and remained for a moment surveying the sparsely populated Edward Kennedy Ellington Concert Hall. Determined that there should be no repetition of previous disturbances, he had decreed that, although the entire solar system might watch the proceedings of the resumed inquiry through the medium of television, the number of persons physically present in the hall should be restricted.

There were differences, too, in the situation of those persons nearer to the center of action. The exclusion of the public having removed the necessity for the protective isolation of the monitor room, Helen and Tom Bruce were seated one on either side of Paul Sharva, at his table on the edge of the central area. Seated at the opposing table, some ten meters to the right, was a massive, bald-headed man with a large hooked nose whom she recognized as Elkan Niebohr, the President of the Excelsior Corporation. As befitted his position, Niebohr was flanked by a corps of secretaries and assistants, but there was no sign of Alger Morton among these people.

Alote Jones began his opening remarks, speaking with measured solemnity. "We are met here this morning in order to make yet a further attempt to reach the truth in this matter. To this end, I understand that Lieutenant Sharva, speaking on behalf of the Space Corps, is now in a position to clarify certain points that were raised by the representative of the Excelsior Corporation. We will therefore call on Lieutenant Sharva."

"Your Honor!" Elkan Niebohr, the television lights glinting on his massive, bald head rose to his feet.

"Mr. Niebohr, we had hoped that the absence of Mr. Morton indicated that the point of view of the Excelsior Corporation in this matter would be handled with greater consideration for public welfare," Alote Jones said severely.

"I beg your pardon, Your Honor," said Niebohr humbly. "But I rise to make a brief statement on behalf of my corporation. If I may be allowed just a few minutes of the court's time?"

"Here we go again!" growled Tom Bruce cynically as Judge Jones conferred with the members of his judiciary.

Paul Sharva darted a glance at him and shook his head, scowling. "Please, Commander!" he whispered urgently.

"Very well, Mr. Niebohr," said Alote Jones. "But be brief."

"Thank you, Your Honor," Niebohr said. "There are two main points. One is that the Board of Directors of the Excelsior Corporation have asked me to offer their apologies to yourself and the judiciary of this inquiry for the manner in which the corporation's interest in this matter has been represented. They ask me to state further that they hold nothing but distaste for the methods used by our erstwhile legal representative, Mr. Alger Morton, and wish to disassociate themselves entirely from these methods, which were completely without consultation or permission."

There was a slight murmuring from the court as Judge Jones said: "Am I to understand, Mr. Niebohr, that the Excelsior Corporation wishes to withdraw all evidence that has been offered on its behalf throughout these proceedings?"

"Save where that evidence refers to matters of incontrovertible fact and is corroborated by the testimony of Space Corps experts, yes, Your Honor," Niebohr said. He turned slightly, his hawk face looking toward the table where Bruce, Sharva and Lindstrom sat. "Secondly, the Excelsior Corporation offers its apologies to the

Space Corps and the officer mainly concerned in the *Athena* affair, Lieutenant Commander Bruce, whose career has been placed in considerable jeopardy by certain allegations made in this courtroom, and elsewhere, by Mr. Morton. I refer particularly to the presentation of confidential Corps documents from the record of Commander Bruce, and obtained by the use of very dubious methods. These matters should never have been introduced into the present proceedings and should be regarded as completely irrelevant to any discussion of the loss of the ill-fated *Athena*."

"Mr. Niebohr, I accept your apology on behalf of the judiciary. It will be entered in the record, accordingly. However, I do not have the authority to speak for the Space Corps, or for Lieutenant Commander Bruce."

Sharva was on his feet. "Your Honor, do I take it that the Excelsior Corporation accepts without reservation our testimony that in destroying the *Athena*, Commander Bruce was acting in the best interests of the population of Earth, in complete and selfless accord with his avowed duty?"

Niebohr inclined his great, domed head. "The Excelsior Corporation accepts that testimony completely, Lieutenant Sharva."

For the first time during the entire proceedings, the solemn features of Judge Alote Jones melted into an expression of something approaching satisfaction. "Then, surely, apart from clearing up certain obscurities which still exist in an interpretation of the motives which caused Hendrik Persoons and his supporters to perform the original act of piracy, the parties concerned have no further testimony to offer?"

"Your Honor, I regret to say that this is not the case," said Paul Sharva grimly. "Although the Space Corps may be prepared to accept the apologies of Mr.

Niebohr on behalf of the Excelsior Corporation, certain irreversible processes have been placed in motion by the very nature of the allegations made by Mr. Morton, through his misguided interpretation of a confidential Corps document. These allegations referred to an incident heretofore classified as top secret in the interests of United Earth. However, it has now been decided that the time is ripe for a full and complete revelation of the facts before the largest possible audience. I have been entrusted with this task, and with your permission, I will proceed."

"I doubt the usefulness of these revelations to the purpose of this inquiry," Alote Jones said.

"That, you may well do, Your Honor," Sharva said with dignity. "But when you have heard and seen the testimony at my disposal, I doubt but that you will admit that it is relevant to the lives and futures of every human being in the known universe."

"A sweeping claim, Lieutenant Sharva."

"It will be substantiated, Your Honor."

Alote Jones conferred with the members of the judiciary while the court waited expectantly. At length, he turned to face the court again. "Very well, Lieutenant Sharva. You may proceed with your testimony."

"Thank you, Your Honor," Sharva said. He opened a file. "To begin, I will first read from a transcript of an official Corps report referring to certain incidents which took place on a Rim Planet known as Minos IV in March of the year 2156. I quote: 'On March 1st, 2156, Lieutenant Bruce, CPO Panos and PO Dockridge were members of the crew of *Venturer Ten* (commanded by Captain Nakamura), which was at the time in orbit around Minos IV. They left the ship aboard a small scout with orders to land on the planetary surface and investigate conditions there. The reason for this expedition was the fact that, since the visit of *Venturer Nine* some eleven years previously, there had been a total absence of communication with the colonists on Minos IV. (At the time of the visit of *Venturer Nine*, the planet's colonist population numbered forty-eight thousand, six hundred human beings, at balanced agriculture and light industrial stage of development.)

" 'Landing first at Minos City, the investigating party found a total absence of life. There were no signs of violence, all the city's buildings were intact, water and electricity supplies, powered by cybernetically controlled atomics, were still working. Everything about the city was normal, except for the complete disappearance of its human inhabitants.

" 'After investigating without success, the party then reboarded the scout and circled the city, surveying carefully. In this way they discovered great scrape marks in the main road which led westward from the city toward the foothills of the mountains known as the Scarpia Range. Following these marks to their conclusion, they landed the scout again and searched on foot. Eventually they found a large cave in a mountainside, the entrance of which had been sealed with a cement-like substance. On hearing noises, they broke down this barrier and discovered within some living creatures.

" 'Upon examination, they came to the conclusion that these creatures had once been human beings, and were, in fact, the total living remnants of the planet's colonist population. Lieutenant Bruce attempted to communicate with these creatures, but found that he could not do so. They had apparently been surgically adapted, altered from their original human form in preparation for a life on a planet where atmospheric and gravity conditions differed materially from those of Earth. Lieutenant Bruce suggested this as the only possible motivation the *nonhuman* surgeons could have had for performing such ghastly modifications, and it would seem to be a logical conclusion. Bruce further suggested that the forty-one creatures found in the cave were in fact the living remnants of unsuccessful attempts at modification. For this reason, he suggested that these unfortunates had not been considered worth the trouble of transportation along with the fifty thousand members of the human population, whose adaptation was presumably satisfactorily completed by the alien surgeons. They were, in a word, rejects.

" 'At length, one creature was found which could still make recognizably human sounds. From its one running eye—I repeat, its eye—it begged to be killed at once; it screamed and clawed with malformed limbs, attempting to take the officer's weapon with the unmistakable intention of killing itself. Faced with this situation, Lieutenant Bruce decided that he could best serve humanity by putting these unfortunate creatures out of their misery. This he did himself, not wishing to involve either of the noncommissioned officers in what he considered a personal decision. (It is understood that PO Dockridge, at least, would have been incapable of assisting in any such action, as he was completely overcome by his experiences in the cave, and CPO Panos was mainly occupied in caring for his needs.)' "

Lieutenant Sharva lowered the file and glanced around the courtroom, whose inhabitants maintained a shocked silence.

"A terrible story," he said grimly. "But its implications are even more terrible and far-reaching. By reading part of this document to you, I have made a beginning only. I am now permitted to show this court, and those who are watching its proceedings on television, totally authentic pictures of some of the creatures found by Lieutenant Bruce and his companions when they broke down the sealing of that cave on Minos IV. I should add that those lacking a strong stomach would be better not to watch what follows. Evidence programmer, may we have the first picture, please?"

There was a brief moment of waiting; it was a tense moment, as though the millions and millions of anxious watchers were making their presence felt in the courtroom. Then a picture appeared on the giant screen at the back of the stage. The watchers in the court gasped; an usher, unprepared, made a retching noise and hurried to a nearby doorway. After the first shocked intake of breath the great hall was silent save for the voice of a television cameraman who cried, totally without blasphemy, "Oh, Christ in heaven!"

Sharva remained dark and composed, as if knowing that the awful strength of his position would best be served by a deliberately unemotional approach. "I will now read to you a digest of information supplied by the Med/Psyche branch of Space Corps, who investigated fully the mutilated cadavers that were transported in deep freeze to Earth. 'There were two types of experimental adaptation. This first example is believed to be derived from a male member of the species *Homo sapiens* and produced by techniques of living surgery far superior to anything at present attempted or contemplated on Earth. It seems that this creature is designed as a kind of workhorse, and that detailed physical reorganization has been carried out with this end in view. The lung capacity has been doubled by grafting, the genitals have been removed, the eyes have been removed and replaced by one, the one being enlarged by some unknown process, and the constituent parts so reassembled that the creature would be able to see in very dim light. It will be observed that the arms are now triple-jointed, and the length of the fingers has been increased by about six centimeters, while the number of digits has been increased to eight. The musculature of the chest and back—which is where the alien surgeons failed in this instance—is an attempt to create a being with enormous lifting powers and great tractile strength.

" 'The second type of experimentation falls into two parts. One is a development of the human female for the purposes of the aliens.' This female, you will observe . . ."

The picture on the screen changed. This time the sounds of revulsion from the people watching were more pronounced. There were some, who after a first glance, covered their eyes and turned away from the unbearable obscenity.

"This female, you will observe," continued Sharva, "has been so altered that she can best serve the function of a reproductive animal. I need say no more about this; the picture speaks for itself."

Sharva waited, and let them—and the millions of television watchers—look hard. Behind him he could hear Helen sobbing, but he did not turn. This was his time to be resolute, to forget his own humanity in the interest of a greater duty.

"And finally," Paul Sharva said, "we come to the third variety . . ."

The picture appeared; Admiral Mariano covered his face, Elena Marx was weeping openly. And, to everyone's amazement, Judge Alote Jones lost his self control. Banging his gavel he called: "Take that picture off! Take it off, instantly!"

The evidence programmer obeyed the command and the picture disappeared. Paul Sharva waited. The humming of the electronic paraphernalia of the television technicians seemed to emphasize the numbed silence that enveloped the hall and its occupants.

"Your Honor, these pictures of the creatures from Minos IV—creatures which, I must emphasize, were *once* human—are not shown with any intention of sensationalism," said Sharva grimly. "But in order to show that somewhere in that vast blackness which every Corpsman fears and respects, no matter how great his or her personal bravery, there lies an extra danger, a new *dimension* of fear. We do not know what these aliens are, where we shall face them, or what their intentions are, but having seen the results of their handiwork on these few, pathetic grotesques left behind them on Minos IV, we can be sure that they are not human in any sense of the word. What happened to the other fifty thousand and more colonists, we can only surmise; and what plans these aliens may have for any other members of the human race they may meet must remain a mystery. Perhaps, with new and better communication techniques, better defences, such a tragedy may never happen to us again.

"However, one thing is clear. There used to be a saying: 'The stars are neutral.' In truth, had we known it, the stars ceased to be neutral long before the day that Lieutenant Bruce made his dreadful discovery on Minos IV. Since that time Space Corps ships have been tirelessly searching for the truth about these alien beings. Previously, nothing more than a half-serious legend, a stock Space Corps joke—the 'Kilroys'—they are now known to be a grim, if unseen, reality.

"Years ago, when nation warred against nation here on Earth, there were armed camps in many lands. Those days are long past, but now the entire empire of United Earth must be, in spirit, and in fact, *one* armed camp, looking up in apprehension toward skies which can no longer be regarded as ours exclusively, skies which we now know we share with an alien race whose motives and actions are, as yet, beyond our comprehension. We look upward, and for the first time we must in truth hear what the poet spoke of as 'the thunder of stars.' "

Sharva paused for a moment and looked squarely at Helen, as though gaining strength from the sight of her proud beauty and the love in her eyes.

"Your Honor," he continued. "I do not propose to take up much more of the court's time. You, and our great audience, have seen the pictures and heard the facts with which we must all learn to live from now on. With regard to the role of Lieutenant Commander Bruce in the *Athena* affair, I would merely say that this officer was confronted with a difficult decision in the face of which any lesser man would have hesitated; the price of such hesitation would have been the death of not five hundred people, but millions, when the *Athena* plunged, a man-made meteor, into the heartland of Northern America. As to his role on Minos IV . . ." Sharva's voice now thundered from his gigantic chest, for the first time approaching something like its full power. "He made a decision there, too. And I ask you, which one of you, had he the necessary courage, would not have done exactly as Bruce did? In those terrible circumstances, you could surely not have done more, or less. And, it cannot be denied, when the implications of that dreadful discovery on Minos IV are considered, that men like Commander Bruce—the men of the Space Corps—are the ones who must constitute United Earth's first defense and shield against the day when we finally meet the alien enemy face to face. Thank your God today for the existence of such men, for tomorrow, or the next day, or many years from now, they will remain your protectors, your guardians of light!"

Lieutenant Paul Sharva bowed with dignity to the judiciary and resumed his seat amid a silence that held a special, charged quality of approval that was more expressive than any standing ovation. In front of their television screens, countless millions wept and felt a new glow of pride in the knowledge of their own humanity. Sharva had said all there was to be said.

Judge Alote Jones, in his wisdom, sensed this. Leaning forward close to the microphone, he spoke briefly to the evidence programmer.

A moment later a solid roll of drums issued from the stereo speakers which lined the interior of the concert hall.

The Judge and the entire court stood rigidly to attention as a recording of the massed bands of the Space Corps playing the anthem of United Earth filled the great building.

She rolled away from him.

"What is it?"

"Must light another stinkpot or we shall have the mosquitoes back." She picked up another of the fragrant little candles and put it to windward. Then she paused, looking out over the lake.

The inquiry was over for Helen and Paul. On Monday she would be back on duty at the shipyard, but tonight and tomorrow they were free—free to swim, cook food and make love on the little beach in the moonlight.

She heard a click, and a faint scuffle behind her. She turned. "Paul?"

The moonlight made his body darker at the same time that it made hers seem lighter. He said: "The camera."

"What?"

"I took a picture of you. Do you mind? I wanted . . ."

The way he broke off told her what was in his mind. She felt at once very sad and tender. Moving across, the sand soft beneath her bare feet, she took his hand. "How many shots have you left?"

"Ten."

"Take ten, then. No, take some of me and then I'll take some of you." For the long, lonely nights, out there in the big dark, she thought. For the hard days, under alien suns, when there is no longer your love to comfort me, my darling. For the years ahead, to remind me that once I was a real woman.

"There's an automatic. We can have some of the two of us together."

A pine had fallen from its meager anchorage and lay tilted into the water. She climbed upon it and sat down, her arms straight by her sides and a little to the rear, her head up toward the stars. "Like this?"

"That's beautiful." He took a picture. "And another. There."

"You don't want me to put any clothes on?"

"Come down." He caught her as she slid off the tree, and held her close.

"The camera!" she said.

"The sand is soft," he said, embracing her. "In any case, I don't want pictures, I want *you*." The male smell of his body mingled with the smell of pines, of summer flowers. "Not just for now, or tomorrow."

She closed his mouth with her own, half-ashamed of herself for using a loving action in this way, as a means of delaying the words that must be said. When the kiss was ended, she broke gently from his embrace and moved back to the beach. He picked up the camera and followed her.

She sat, hands clasped about her knees, looking up at him as he approached, and prayed for strength. He was very beautiful in the moonlight, a dark giant, standing straight and true, the lake silver and velvet behind him.

"We have to talk," he said gently. "About our sons . . ."

"Paul, please." His very gentleness was an agony inside her.

"You've decided?" He knelt in the sand, his face about a meter from hers.

"I owe the Corps . . ."

"Your *womanhood*?"

"Paul, after what you said in court today, how can I resign my commission? Everyone will be needed. It would be like desertion."

"Nothing has changed."

"How can you say that? Minos IV, those horrible . . . things."

"It all happened ten years ago."

"And tomorrow, the next day, when we meet *them* face to face?"

"Then it will be time enough to make sacrifices. For now, perhaps even more, there must be time to live." He moved toward her.

"No! Don't come closer, please," she said. "I have to think."

"There are a thousand officers with your training and qualifications, but only one mother for our sons," he said.

"The honest lawyer . . . Damn you, Paul!" she said, choking back the tears that misted her eyes.

"Special pleading." He moved forward and took her in his arms, pulling her toward him.

Her chin lay for a moment on his shoulder, and she looked up at the sky. The stars were scattered like a glittering powder, beckoning, awesome. She closed her eyes and nuzzled her face down into the dark warmth of his chest, hearing the strong, regular beating of his heart.

"I'll see Admiral Carter on Monday," she said.

THUNDER OF STARS

. . . We know it's all absurd,
Bandied about over centuries, that word.
And yet, it's not all piss and smoke.
Watch 'em laugh, when they say, "Kilroy
was here."
Hear that laugh, man.
Smell the sweat of fear.

(KILROY : I. Kavanin.)

THE PERT sub-Lieutenant in Rear Admiral Carter's office got a reply from her chief. "The Admiral will see you now, ma'am."

"Thank you." Helen went in and saluted.

"Good morning, Commander." Carter's leathery face seemed almost affable as he looked up at her. "I'm pleased you called in this morning. I've just received confirmation of the appointment of *Venturer Twelve*'s Commander."

"Bruce?" Her heart was beating faster, but she maintained an outward calm.

Carter grinned. "After the way he came out of the *Athena* inquiry, who *else*?"

"I'm glad," she said sincerely. This was what Tom Bruce wanted, his reason for living. It was right for him.

"Makes things easier all round, doesn't it?" Carter said. "You've been a good team before, you will be again."

"No, sir," she said firmly.

He looked up at her, a new sharpness growing in his eyes, his mouth opening to speak.

She anticipated him. "Admiral," she said carefully. "I wish to sign out of the Corps."

Carter restrained himself. He rose to his feet, slowly, head sunk deep between his massive shoulders. "Sit down," he ordered.

He walked to the door and opened it. "Pringle, for the next ten minutes, hold everything. I'm busy."

He shut the door, then walked back to his desk and carefully resumed his seat. He took out a cigar and lit it. He blew out a cloud of smoke, and through it he said: "It sounded just as though you said you wanted to sign out."

"That's what I said, sir."

"Umph . . . Now, shall I just forget you said it and we'll get back to work?"

"I meant it, Admiral."

Carter did a miraculous thing again. He stopped himself swearing and he maintained his voice at a quiet conversational level. "You are an acting Lieutenant-Commander with a citation for bravery. You are twenty-six years old; you are fit, tough and on top of your job, Second in Command of the newest, finest ship the Corps possesses. Just what the hell are you talking about?"

"You heard me, sir."

"With first liftoff only three weeks away, you want to sign out?"

"Yes, sir."

"And leave the Corps completely?"

"Completely."

"Bloody, bastarding hell!" growled the Rear Admiral. "And you really think you mean it?"

"I do mean it."

"Why?"

"Paul Sharva has asked me to marry him."

"Sharva . . . And . . . ?"

"I have accepted."

Carter stuck out his chin like an angry turtle. "You pregnant?"

"No."

He nodded, tight lipped, his eyes glinting. "Well . . . The oldest trick, and you missed out on it."

"I think I can choose when . . ."

"Nuts!" Carter said. "And if you still want to sign out, the answer is no!"

"Admiral, I am entitled . . ."

"To get on with the job you've been trained for," Carter said. "You *can't* sign out. Under the Conservation of Senior Personnel Order, which came into force on the first of this month, it can't be done. You have to give one year's notice, unless pregnant in the case of female officers, in which event duty terminates four months before the birth of the child. *And in any case, you don't love Paul Sharva!*"

"That's not for you to say . . ."

"Bloody hell, girl!" Carter slapped his hands on his desk and shouted, "This is *my* patch of the Corps you're on! Don't you go telling me what I can't do! I have just quoted the regulation to you, and if you're going to get past it in the only way that's left, you'll have to make medical history. Furthermore, I repeat, you just think Sharva is a nice guy. So he is. He'll be Lieutenant Commander in the JAG's branch by the end of the year; unless as I strongly suspect, he's seconded to duty at the Presidential house. He's gentle, he's kind, he's a thoroughly good man; and he'll make a good husband, and a loving father. He's like a great big tame bull; he just needs loving by some affectionate cow of a woman, and that, Helen Lindstrom, is not *you*! You'd be throwing your life away, and more important, you'd be buggering me about in a way I won't have. Get that? I won't *have* it! You are going to lift off on *Venturer Twelve*, and you'll like it! There'll be speeches, and bits on television about far-flung frontiers, and all the folks will cheer like fuck as you go, away for two, three, four years. And, oh boy, I shall be glad to see you *all* go!"

"You'll be glad to . . . ?"

"Of course I shall! I want to get on with *Venturer Thirteen* and you're all in the way! Do you think I'm going to hold up liftoff because of your love life? Get up in the big dark, girl, in a heavy duty suit, smelling your own sweat as you walk on the outside skin, watching the crew—your crew—do a repair. *That's* for you; that's what you signed in for, so don't cheat yourself and think of signing out!" He snorted, looked down at his desk and busied himself with some papers. Half a minute later he looked up fiercely. "Was there something *else*, Lieutenant Commander Lindstrom?"

Her voice was just audible. "No, sir."

He returned the salute as she left. His hand came down and pressed the dialing buttons on his vid. Response was prompt.

"CPO Sun, Records. Good morning, Admiral Carter, sir."

"I want you to take a note of the following amendment to Corps General Orders."

"Sir?"

"Don't gape, man! Get it down!" snapped Carter. "You will give this amendment an appropriate number and back-date it to the first of this month. Heading: 'Conservation of Senior Personnel. Officers of the acting rank of Lieutenant Commander and above, who are on the active list, are required to give one year's notice when wishing to sign out. The only exceptions to this ruling to be Extreme Compassionate Grounds, and in the case of female officers, presentation of Form 447/P through a medical officer. In such cases, signing out date will be four months before the ETA of child.' Got that?"

"But, sir, you can't—I mean, *back-dating*—?"

"Sun," said the admiral gently, "I believe you are up for promotion to warrant officer?"

"Yes, sir."

"And who put you up for that promotion, as a reward for zealous and devoted service?"

"You, sir."

"You'd make a fine warrant officer, Sun," said the admiral. "Think of the pride of your honorable ancestors, eh?"

"Yes, sir."

"Not to mention your dear wife, Kam Lan, and your nine—is it?—children."

"Ten, shortly, sir."

"Well then, think of that pay, CPO Sun."

"Yes, sir."

"And the allowances."

"Yes, sir."

"And don't forget that the number assigned to the amendment must tally with the numberings on the first of the month."

"It will be difficult, sir." Sun's plump, southern Chinese face looked worried.

"Not for a *warrant officer*," the admiral assured him, and terminated the conversation.

He walked over to the wall and looked up at the personnel board for *Venturer Twelve*. There were no empty places now. Each position had its name tag, from Commander down to Crewmen G/D i/c San Duty. He moved across to a rack on his right and picked up a big tube of paper. Unrolling the tube on the surface of a worktable, it revealed itself as a preliminary drawing of *Venturer Thirteen*. Only another few weeks, and he could really get to work on her . . .

The vid beeped. Holding the drawing open, he walked across to his desk.

The caller was his wife. "Junius, I was wondering if there was any chance of . . ."

He let the springy paper roll itself up with a snap. He beamed.

"Honey," said Junius F. Carter, "I'm going to take the rest of the day off. I'll be home for lunch. Tell me then, huh?" He switched off, leaving his wife staring in astonishment at a blank screen.

"Another bourbon on the rocks, Minsky."

"Yes, ma'am." The dapper little steward of the officers' mess moved across and filled the glass. "Too bad about the President. He was a great man."

"One of the greatest," Helen said.

"They say he asked to be buried in space."

"Yes, so I understand."

"Quite an honor for the Corps."

"I guess so."

Finally coming to the conclusion that the Lieutenant Commander was not in a talkative mood, the steward faded toward the other end of the bar.

Helen sat, looking down into the amber depths of her drink, reflecting on the self-torturing mechanism of the human mind that always seemed to insist that what you couldn't have, you wanted all the more.

It was nearly an hour now since she had called Lake Cities and talked to Paul; but her body was still remembering those days and nights at the lakeside, still longing for his gentle, animal strength, for his loving. He had been understanding, as she had expected he would be. All the trite phrases that had been milling around in her head throughout the long day in the shipyard—"a clean break," "duty to the Corps," "best for both of us"—had been mercifully unnecessary. He had sensed her answer from the first moment of seeing her face on his screen and, like the gentle person he was, he had done everything he could to make things easier for her. They had both been very adult and sensible, agreeing that, although she would not be leaving Earth for at least another three weeks, it would be best not to see each other again. A silence, in which she looked deep into his dark eyes and saw the hurt there, two brief good-bys, and the dream was over.

Carter had been right, the wise old bastard. Paul Sharva was a good man, a gentle man; but she was not the placid, affectionate cow of a woman he needed. It wouldn't have lasted; sooner or later she would have looked up at the stars and felt the call and then she would have made life miserable for both of them.

"Good evening, Commander. May I join you?"

She turned her head and faced the angelic smile of Radar Lieutenant Yvonne Maranne. She was twenty-two years old, dark haired and coffee skinned, with bedroom eyes and a curvy-curvy body that would send crewmen mad on a long trip and set them dreaming unattainable dreams.

"Of course. What will you have?"

Helen caught a whiff of strictly off-duty perfume, as Maranne wriggled herself onto the stool.

"A sweet sherry, please."

Of course, it would be a *sweet* sherry. Helen called the steward and ordered.

"How are things going in your department?" Helen asked.

"All systems go," Maranne said, twinkling over the glass, which she held in both hands like a child. This, apparently, was her cultivated off-duty *persona*.

Helen sipped her bourbon.

"I understand that the new Commander is arriving day after tomorrow," Maranne said. "You've worked with him before, haven't you?"

"Yes," Helen said.

"I've only seen pictures of him, of course," Maranne said. "But he looks kind of handsome."

"He is," Helen said. If you like robots, added the voice inside her head.

"They say he was married once."

"Not any more," Helen said.

"How is he with the women officers, I mean . . . ?"

I know precisely what you mean, you curvy little cow, thought Helen. But Tom Bruce wouldn't give you a second look, with your little girl smile and your sugar and spice ways. I know what Tom Bruce likes, and I'll be the one to give it to him, not you.

She downed the rest of her drink quickly, conscious that Maranne was still looking up at her, waiting for the answer to her question.

"The same as he is with the *men* officers. He expects them to get on with the job," she said as she got off the stool.

Lieutenant Maranne's eyes widened at the harshness of her superior officer's tone.

"And one thing, Lieutenant," Helen said.

"Yes, ma'am?"

"Don't ever try to use what you've got between your thighs as an excuse for inefficiency or Tom Bruce will kick you out of the Corps, right on your sweet little arse! Goodnight, Lieutenant."

Outside the officers' mess she slowed her pace, strolling along the tarmac, feeling the cool breeze fingering her hair. Then she stopped walking and stood looking across the shipyard to where the great spheroid of *Venturer Twelve* stood, proud in the light of a hundred arcs. She could see the flashes of welding torches and hear the sound of men and machines working.

She stood there, watching for a long time, and then, as though in response to some soundless thunder, her gaze moved. The night sky was crystal clear. If she reached out her hand, she could plunge it deep into the Milky Way and pluck out a handful of stars. Six stars, one for each of Paul Sharva's sons.

She realized with a surge of anger that tears were streaming hotly down her cheeks. And yet, it was not *she* who was crying, but someone else, buried deep down inside, a woman who might have been weeping for her unborn children.

The collaboration between Dan Morgan and John Kippax began over twenty years ago when they were both professional guitarists, and has continued through a number of collaborative writing efforts since. They have both been writing science fiction for a number of years but this novel and *Seed of Stars*, also published in Pan Books, are their first combined efforts in this field. Two more titles, *The Neutral Stars* and *Where No Stars Guide*, will be published by Pan in 1975.